THE BIG STIFFS

The President of the United States sent his very Special Private Investigator, Ed Noon, to Rome to pick up an innocuous package. But the enigma of that package and what it held hurled the redoubtable Noon into a fantastic set-piece of espionage, mayhem and sudden death. Where else but the Eternal City could he have met a pistol-packing giant like Kate Arizona, a tough policeman like Captain Santini, and the dread terrorist group known as the Arcangeli?

MICHAEL AVALLONE

THE BIG STIFFS

Complete and Unabridged

LINFORD
Leicester

First published in Great Britain in 1977 by
Robert Hale Limited
London

First Linford Edition
published 1998
by arrangement with
Robert Hale Limited
London

British Library CIP Data

Avallone, Michael
    The big stiffs.—Large print ed.—
Linford mystery library
    1. Detective and mystery stories
    2. Large type books
    I. Title
    813.5'4 [F]

ISBN 0–7089–5340–9

Published by
F. A. Thorpe (Publishing) Ltd.
Anstey, Leicestershire

Set by Words & Graphics Ltd.
Anstey, Leicestershire
Printed and bound in Great Britain by
T. J. International Ltd., Padstow, Cornwall

This book is printed on acid-free paper

There have been some incredible giants who have distinguished and purified the Italian *ethos* by somehow making it clearer and less misunderstood all over the world. Thereby obliterating the Borgia poison, the *Mafia* machine gun, the cowardly soldier and *pasta*-fattened *mamas* and *papas* of low comedy, from the consciousness of the universe.

It's a long walk from Dante and Michelangelo and Galileo to the laboratories of Marconi and Fermi and the outfield of Joe Di Maggio.

Frank Capra's camera, as well as De Sica's and Fellini's are golden statues besides those of Caruso, Toscanini and Lanza.

Rome is dying, now, as I see it, and perhaps this book may be able to show a little of the Why. But, affectionately and lovingly, it is dedicated to the Arts of Italy and, of course, to the unique lady of the cinema — the one and only Sophia Loren.

Personaggi principali:
. . . according to the Italian dictionary

ED NOON
agente speciale
MICHELE SANTINI
inspettore di Roma
HUGO, ALFREDO, GINO
carabinieri
JOY DEVEAU
una ragazzina bella
FLOOD
funzionario dell' U.S. Embassy
KATE ARIZONA
ragazza-spia
THE CHIEF
presidente degli Stati Uniti
THE 'ARCANGELI'
Mafiosi
ROMA
La Citta Eternale

. . . and some of them lose something
in the translation.

1

Up the Godfather

'To that High Capital, where kingly Death Keeps his pale court in beauty and decay,
He came . . . '
>> Shelley, in his elegy dedicated to Keats.

The Italian police official was someone I had seen in every moviemaker's idea of just what an Italian police official should look like. He was bandit-moustached, broad-shouldered, bombastically proud and on the verge of acquiring a corporation behind the shining Sam Browne belt buckle girdling his waist. His eyes were midnight black, expressive and snapping and he couldn't talk without using his hands. For extras, he was voluble, excessively polite and obviously disinclined to wound my feelings with nasty, suspicious questions about the true nature of my visit to his beloved Roma. But he was on to me about something.

He was maybe ten years younger than Marcello Mastroianni but he wore his weariness just as well.

Whatever he really was, I seemed to be in trouble.

His office was a cramped, tiny sweat-box, without air-conditioning, located two floors up from the sun-bleached, rotting sidewalk. The station house seemed to be situated in one of the rattier corners of *la bella Roma*. A personal observation I was not about to voice aloud. I still have relatives living in Italy.

We were alone because he seemed to want it that way. And maybe two minutes after he confiscated my U.S. passport, New York ID and PI card and licence, he was scowling broadly at sight of the .45 Colt automatic lying on the desk before him, which one of his younger, less polite, uniformed subordinates had briskly frisked from my shoulder harness.

He was now also in possession of a

5 × 8 thick, brown leather book of mine which he held up between his manicured fingers and dangled accusingly. In my face, as it were. As if it were something pornographic like *Eight Nights In A Brothel*.

'This is yours, *Signor*?'

'You know it is.'

'*Prego*. Answer my question.'

'You saw your boy bring it into this office, lay it on your desk and say right out loud in perfect English: 'I removed this article from the Signor's room at the Villa Del Parco, one ten Via Nomentana at exactly ten hundred hours this morning — ' Stop playing games, Inspector.'

'I am a *Capitano*, *Signor*. A Captain. *Prego* — please. I must ask. You must answer. These matters must be handled in a suitable manner. So there is no question later of any violation of rights. You understand, I trust?'

'Yes.' I nodded to show him there were no hard feelings. But the chair I was sitting in was getting hotter by the second. 'Or rather I think I do.

3

You've had me arrested after searching my rooms, brought me here to this office, subjected me to a body frisk and not once have I screamed about my legal rights or demanded that you call the American Embassy. All very high-handed, Captain. Wouldn't you agree?'

'*Ah!*' His dark eyes twinkled and enormous self-satisfaction rippled over his swarthy face. 'Just so. You have come right to the point. And I, simple official that I am, must confess to extreme confusion and surprise that you have behaved in the manner which you so aptly describe.'

'Come again?' I stalled.

'Why do you *not* speak up for your rights, *Signor*?'

'I'm not throwing my tourist weight at you for a very good reason. I'm rather a student of police procedure all over the world and I do want to see how far you'll take this routine. My education about Italia is sadly neglected.'

I was lying and he somehow knew that, too.

It was in his dark eyes lighting up

like twin cigarette lighters firing. An appreciative smile made the tips of his blossoming, bold moustache fold upward. Jerry Colonna style.

He tapped the brown book triumphantly with a firm forefinger.

'Perhaps the reason for your charitable conduct is in this book, *Signor*. Your journal. Diary, as you would say. Even a simple scan-through of the pages of the past few days, would seem to suggest that you are not quite the simple *Americano* you pretend to be.'

'There's no law against keeping a diary.'

'Of course, there is not. But this particular diary and its most specific details about certain matters again suggests something else. Something, let us say, far less innocent than merely words and notes about my country. Come, my friend. Do not waste the time with me. You know what I refer to.'

'Sorry,' I said, staring him straight in the eye. 'You'll have to spell that out. I don't know what you're talking about.'

'Don't you?'

5

The smile had gone from his face, the politeness took a flying jump through the steaming office window. The unbearable heat of the day, coupled with everything else that was on the Captain's mind, made his next statement something right out of the old Perry Mason TV programme. The hot, flaming accusation came slamming across the desk that separated us, leaving fear wherever it touched. He didn't miss an inch of my vulnerable hide.

'As representative of the Italian Government, Signor Noon, and accredited police official of the City of Rome, I duly notify you that you are under arrest as a spy. Since this comes under the jurisdiction of the Military, you shall be turned over to the Army as soon as we are able to contact them. There is no further use in denials or lame stories and alibis, *Signor*. The diary you saw fit to maintain as a record of your activities is quite enough proof for this office. It will be necessary to get in touch with your Embassy since these are very serious charges. But, before that, may

6

I respectfully suggest that you make a statement and thereby reduce feelings of ill-will and hostility that your presence has already engendered in the men of my command? It will go much better for you if you do. Believe me, *Signor*. I mean that most sincerely.'

'You're crazy,' I finally managed to blurt, getting out from under the tremendous sense of absurdity I was feeling. 'And I mean *that*, most sincerely.'

His face flushed, his shoulders hunched and he dropped the brown book on the desk. Its thump was like the fall of an axe. An executioner's axe. Somewhere across the back of my neck.

'This attitude will not serve you well — ' he began sternly, as if imploring me to be a good spy and make a clean breast of the whole dirty business. 'I deplore your activities, naturally, as a Roman, but if there are mitigating circumstances — '

'Captain,' I said very slowly, very carefully. 'There is nothing in that diary that can even come close to what you're accusing me of. You've misinterpreted something. Maybe some of my American slang — '

'No, *Signor*. I assure you I have not.' His eyes glittered. A four-aces glitter that suddenly made me feel like I was holding a pair of deuces in a life-or-death card game. Suddenly, he nudged the brown diary across his desk at me. 'There. Read for yourself. Go ahead. I dare you. And then tell me I imagine things. You need only concern yourself with the entries from the eighteenth of July through to yesterday — the twenty fifth, I believe. You will see for yourself, I think, just how you condemn yourself from your own mouth. *Prego*. Do as I tell you. Perhaps it will convince you that this lying and prevarication all comes to nothing.'

Stupefied, I reached for the diary.

He seemed so rock-bottom sure, so dead certain.

There had to be some kind of mistake.

He couldn't have blithely stumbled over my cover. Not this simple, officious Captain of the Carabinieri.

I was a spy, all right.

But not the spy he meant. Not the type

8

he might be looking for. I hadn't come in from the cold. My business in Roma had nothing to do with Italy per se.

I had nothing against Italy. Not even spaghetti Westerns. And any country which can lay claim to Da Vinci, Michelangelo, Caruso, Toscanini, Fermi and Sophia Loren has to have something going for it at all times in the credit department. Those are far too many winners to pass off as just a bunch of lucky breaks.

Even as I picked up the brown leather diary, riffling the pages to the designated dates, I was trying to remember where I could have slipped up — indeed, if I had slipped up at all.

The dark glittering eyes of the Captain seated behind the desk, no more than two yards away, never left my face.

Those eyes might have been the black bores of two rifles lined up, ready, waiting, and thoroughly capable of destruction.

As steaming and hot as the Roma day was, I felt cold.

My .45 on the desk was toothless. The

clip had been removed.

Strapped to the Captain's Sam Browne belt was a holstered pistol just a little smaller than a siege gun. Close to his hand.

I wasn't going to give him a chance to use it.

Or an excuse, either.

Quietly, without moving a muscle, I read my own diary.

For better or for worse.

Or both.

And mostly for my own edification.

I didn't expect to be entertained.

I wasn't.

2

The Marble Morgue

'I admire human Nature but I do not like Men — I should like to compose something honourable to Man . . . '

John Keats,
November 1820 – February 1821

18 Tuesday July (Martedi)
Arrivederci, Rapallo and Hello, Roma. The Rome Express *(Rapido)* was the usual clutter of crowded aisles and Italian *non-sequiturs*. Pisa's *campanile* (bell-tower) leaned very briefly as we whizzed through that foggy town. My coach fellow-traveller was Carlo, a 25 year old student, earning extra money to augment his studies by hiring himself out to deliver a limousine to Rome for some African Embassy official. I practised my Italian on him. He in turn used what

little English he knew. Roma *Termini* (the Station) was *enormo*. Porters, cabs, tourists, in droves. Hit the Villa del Parco, 110 Via Nomentana at 3:30. Nice hotel set back from the street, up a long path. Quiet, secluded layout. Got a fine room on the ground floor, just back of the lobby. Hope my *lira* holds out.

19 Wednesday July (Mercoledi)

In hot, glaring sunlight, Rome's dirty, bleached marble and stone is *molto* depressing. *Molto!* Ditto hard-to-get taxis, too much walking to get anywhere and an eternal rat race of miniature autos, bikes and scooters. Went to the Colosseum and it was not disappointing, as the guide books tend to indicate. How could such a fabled, storied monster be a bust, even if it's sort of Shea Stadium with holes? Dug it all the way — excavations and all. The Roman Forum close by is almost an overgrown cow pasture now. The huckster guides and Roman sharpshooters out to trim the tourists are very non-*simpatico*. Beat after the Colosseum, found a Snack Bar on the winding hill above the Termini. Every cab I tried to flag down was 'going back to the garage!' Finally cornered one and returned to the Villa Del Parco. Walked down the Via Del Corso to the Fontana di Trevi, after sundown. Tossed in some coins, made some wishes and wondered where all the hookers and streetwalkers were hiding. Every doll I saw looked young, lovely and just — nice. Hard to tell, though. Rome seems best seen at night. It's cooler and looks less like a whore the way it does in broad daylight.

20 Thursday July (Giovedi)

Vatican City at last. Over the bridge. A young daredevil *autista* cabdriver zipped me to St. Peter's, which is merely astounding. Roma has a lot but nothing else like this old church. Michelangelo's Rotunda work is really fantastic, and of course, Cappella Sistina (the many signs drove me nuts) is impossible to describe. Hard to assimilate in a noisy, throbbing tourist mob. Lunched at Paolo's outside the *Musee* (museum), still thinking what

13

a One-Man-Monument St. Peter's really is. Back to the hotel, with the solution on how to handle Roma. You tour in the morning and the evening only, so that in the night you can enjoy the city. Afternoons are out, definitely. Everything closes after two, the natives take their siesta and all bets are off. Down to the Spanish Steps after dark. The Keats-Shelley Room, overlooking the high staircase, was closed. Bernini's bark (The Tub) is in sad shape below, at the base of the steps. Cracked, chipped and just a water fountain for the thirsty idlers. Dined at Nino's, a good, inexpensive *ristorante*. Ate spaghetti *dalla Bolognesa* — delicious.

21 Friday July (Venerdi)
Spanish Steps again. American Express is right down the street. Exchanged some travellers' checks for more *lira*. Dropped into the Keats-Shelley Room. Excellent and fascinating cubbyhole in the middle of madness. Keats' last four months of life must have been horrible. Living with such beauty and dying by inches.

Walked to the top of the Steps, past all the young Hippies with their guitars, long hair and sidewalk pitch-concessions at each landing, and found the Via Veneto. Lunch at the Cafe de Paris, air-conditioned and great. The Borghese Gardens, Rome's Central Park, is just at the end of the *ristorante*-crowded street. Took a half-hour hike through the woods. Rain threatened again but *pioggia* never seems to come. Not in Roma. Took a ride back to the Colosseum and watched the legions of starved, ugly cats parading in the ghostly moonlight over the ancient pile of rocks. Tourists galore again but still sort of isolated. Then back to Via Veneto again for a late evening *cappuccino* with the *La Dolce Vita* set. Fellini was right. Boredom lives on the Via Veneto. In very expensive clothes.

22 Saturday July (Sabato)

Giardino Zoologico, a zoo like all the other zoos the world over. Fed the mandrills, the goats and the antelopes. Saw a cat roaming the merry-go-round area with her about-to-be-born kitten dangling from her hind legs. Oldtimer told me dead kittens are all over the zoo. The oppressive, muggy heat drops them like flies. Can believe that. Roma: *Three o'clock* is a Sunday town, every day of the week. Traffic and people seem to simply disappear, only to materialise after six o'clock. Checked out the Via Veneto again, after dining at Doney's. At the sidewalk tables, same faces all the time. Same kinds of faces — *i.e.* tourist, native, expatriate and mostly — *BORED*. The Veneto cabbies, who line up around the corner like a fleet, seem to be Roma's true sharpshooters. All out for the hustle and the con and the buck. The U.S. Embassy building right across the street where the hill starts down seems out of place. Quiet and orderly. Though the neighbourhood abounds in high-priced luxury hotels. Got a laugh. Private Detectives advertise all over the buildings with huge, gaudy signs. Ditto the cover of the Roma phone book. Went back to the Colosseum again, before taking the long ride back to the Villa del Parco. Nobody bothers me there. The desk men don't ask any questions, the maids are all polite and I've had no interference of any kind, so far. So good!

23 Sunday July (Domenica)
SPQR — the Italian brand is tattooed over everything. Sidewalks, gratings, fountains, garbage pails. Visited the Piazza del Campidoglio, up behind the Vittorio Emanuele. Great busts and statues prevail in the Museum but the Tintoretto canvases (*The Maddelena is great*) dominate here. *Molto humido esta giorno*, as my cabdriver said. It is — a scorcher, today. Brief thunderstorm at six cooled off the city. Then everything heated up again. Went to the Piazza Navona, dined at Tres Scalini on purely heavenly shrimp and watched the art exhibition in the plaza. Then located the Pantneon where the dark and gloomy Agrippa Temple lords it over a narrow plaza. Met a teenage college female named Joy Deveau who was hiking over Europe for the Summer. Seemed to be a sharp gal, with quiet good looks. I played

the wiser, older brother and bought her a coke and then went back to the hotel. Alone. Still haven't found what I came here for. Maybe I never will . . .

★ ★ ★

I looked up from the diary, confused. And perspiring.

The Captain was still staring at me. Poised, expectant, a tight smile again playing with the ends of the bandit moustache.

'Time,' I said. 'You sure you aren't reading between the lines, my Captain? There is nothing here to suggest anything but a lonely, romantic, over-aged American trying to find a little excitement in your fair Roma — '

'No,' he said, firmly, without raising his voice. 'Read on, *Signor*. When you are done — I see you have two more entries — is that not so? — then I will show you what your writing tells me in my professional capacity. *Capisce, Signor?*'

There was no need to answer him. He

had all the ideas and all the high cards.
I read on, anxious to be done with his
game. Whatever it was, whatever he felt
sure it might be.

24 Monday July (Lunedi)

Monday morning in Roma. Cars,
bikes, dust, noise. Bedlam. Fiats all over
town. Back to the Spanish Steps again.
Re-visited the Keats-Shelley Room. Vera
Cacciatore was in this time. Back from
her Venetian holiday. Incredibly young-
looking for a woman who has minded
the store for more than thirty years. As
custodian and scholar. Her name means
'hunter'. We talked about New York and
the Government and the War. Signed
the Guest Book and left. Went back to
the Fontana di Trevi. A bosomy Italian
girl was imitating Anita Ekberg dancing
half-naked in the water. She scrammed
before two carabinieri could arrest her.
Gaping tourists enjoyed the show. Dined
in the Federalino (built in 1835) which
is only yards from the fountain's edge.
Poker-faced waiters, suspicious middle-
aged matron-tourists had a spirited

argument. A fist fight broke out in the *piazza* itself. After dinner, I walked past the Vittorio Emanuele, toward the Colosseum. Still Shea Stadium, Swiss-cheese style, but a great spot after dark. The cats were out in hordes, being fed by the tourist kids and their families. The moon tonight was bigger than Texas. No mail or messages from home, yet.

25 Tuesday July (Martedi)
Last hours in the Villa del Parco. Had to knock off the day so did it in grand style. Off to St. Pietro's in Vincoli to see the *Moses* of Michelangelo. Truly unique. Another impossible-to-describe masterpiece. Then on to St. Mary's in Cosmedia where that odd wall panel, *Bocca della Verita* (The Mouth Of Truth) is. Aped Gregory Peck and Audrey Hepburn in *Roman Holiday*. You stick your arm in the mouth of the horned demon face and you don't get your arm back if you tell a lie. Have to put some notes here — *senza burro* means without butter — *camera* is room; *senso unico* — one way; *aranciata* is orangeade; *vieta*

to means prohibited — *dové il gabinetto?* is where's the john? More later —

★ ★ ★

The next page, somehow now damningly blank, stopped me.

I shut the book, only aware of two things. The Captain's fixed, waiting smile and the low hum of slowly-rotating fan blades above our heads, trying to cool the tiny, crowded room. There was no point in reading on. There was no more to read. I had stopped making entries on 25 July Tuesday. *(Martedì)*.

Dear Diary, Roma style, was ended.

A bewildered stare was all I had for the weary police official waiting patiently for my response. On the other side of the desk.

'So,' I said, *'what?'*

'So,' he countered, shaking his head sadly. 'You see nothing then? You continue to show great innocence, eh? Very well, dear Signor Noon. I, Captain Michele Santini, will educate you somewhat. We are not so provincial here in

21

Roma, as you might think. We know things. We keep up with the news. *Allora*, we know something of you. Who you are and what you are in that great big United States of yours. The *detectivo privato* — involved all too often in murder cases, world affairs and many times you have put your big foot in those matters which are usually the business of secret agents and — shall we say, enemies? *Espionage, Signor!'*

'Lay off the plurals, Captain.' I got some wind back into my sails, still not knowing what he was leading up to in his slow Continental way. 'Speak for yourself, Giovanni.'

'Michele,' he corrected me, proudly, missing the gag completely. His dark eyes contracted and the smile vanished. The bandit moustache straightened out, fiercely. And somehow the whole routine was startlingly familiar, now. *Déjà vu* in spades. There was a Captain Mike back in New York Homicide who this Captain Michele did not have to take a back seat to. They were both chips off the old police block. Grim, remorseless, one-track minded. This was literally the same man, Italian Style. Coppers under the skin.

'All right. Captain Michele. You tell me what you think you have on me and then maybe I can laugh in your face.'

'I do not think you will laugh at all, *Signor*. Perhaps, you will be crying, eh? All the way to our strongest prison.' He picked up the brown diary, balancing it on the big flat palm of his left hand. His patient frown was not unkind, somehow. It was if as if he could not believe what he had found in the entries. 'Very well. To the specifics. You have been in Rome exactly eight days. Nine, to be precise, if we count today. And we cannot fail to do that, can we? According to your own hand, you were supposed to leave yesterday. You did not. The *first* cause for suspicion. We know much of your activities, *now*. Thanks to your diary-habit and the necessary investigation following your arrest. You arrived here in Rome on the *Rapido* from Rapallo. We know you stayed at the Excelsior on the Mediterranean for a lonely period of three days. That, it seems, came directly following a one week visit to Paris. You had arrived there by jet plane. Orly Airport from New York in your America. You seem to have very little luggage, Signor, for a man on European holiday of such long duration. One suitcase, a black attaché bag. And an assortment of rather interesting weapons for a peaceful tourist, I should think.'

'I'm not a clotheshorse,' I interrupted quickly. 'I didn't intend to swim on the Riviera or take in any night life. So I don't need a tuxedo. I always travel light. And that's no crime. Unless you belong to the Beautiful People. And I certainly don't. As for the weapons — ' I shrugged. 'It's a cruel, unfriendly world, isn't it?'

He pounced on that, eagerly, still holding the diary.

'*Si, Signor*. The weapons, by all means. I wish to know why a man visits *la bella Roma* with a virtual arsenal of death at his very fingertips!'

'Take it easy, Captain. I'm duly licensed and authorised. For that Colt right there and every little toy in my

24

suitcase. I'll admit plastic explosives and cigarette lighter pistols and my gas pellets are a bit much but — I need them in my line of work.'

'But how did you get them through customs, my friend?'

'I can't tell you that. Let's say I have influence.'

'Let's say you *must* tell me. For what you carry about your person so recklessly has everything to do with the charges we intend to hold you for. Think about that and think well before you answer, *Signor*. No amount of political secrecy or diplomatic intervention from your Embassy can gloss over the possession of such toys, as you say. The diary alone will damn you!'

He slammed it down in the desk again. This time it didn't sound like an axe falling. More like a ton of TNT. And the habitual weariness had faded from him. He was worked up, now. Passionate and unforgiving. And I still didn't understand him. Or what he had on me.

'Then you stop stalling too, Captain. What do you find in my diary that makes such fascinating reading?'

Controlling himself and nodding, eyes glinting at me, he played drumming rhythms with his hands and hit me with his news of the day. The week. And the year. It wasn't at all what I expected.

'Signor Noon,' Captain Michele Santini said very evenly, very coldly and unargumentatively, as though it were the Gospel according to Pope Paul, 'during the time you have spent in this city, you have visited many places. The Colosseum, the Piazza Navona, St. Pietro's, St. Mary's in Cosmedia, Vincoli, the Villa Borghese — a great many of our traditional and most loved 'tourist' attractions. I will not name all the places you have been. Those I speak of are sufficient. *Allora* — what will you say, *Signor*, when I tell you that explosive contraptions — lethal devices — were found at each and everyone of the sites you visited — all within hours of your visits? You must be a very poor saboteur, my friend, to have your handiwork so easily discovered. But — even that — which is monstrous and for which I myself would have you stoned

26

to death in front of the Vittorio Emauele at high noon — is not all. The lady you speak of so endearingly on the evening of July the twenty third, this Signorina Deveau — in your own words — *a sharp gal, with quiet good looks*? — well, Signor Noon. She was found before dawn in the very waters of the Fontana di Trevi by the maintenance people who clean the place after the coarse tourists have departed.' He stared across the desk at me with all the contempt there is in this world. 'She was drowned. Very violently. Very brutally. And there are evidences of an ugly sexual assault. Must I say more?'

'No,' I said. 'Not just this second. That's quite enough for openers. Let me think, will you — '

'Think hard, *Signor*. I intend to prosecute you to the limit of my powers. With, I should add, the greatest of pleasure.'

I couldn't blame him at all. Not hardly.

By his standards, the man sitting on the other side of his Police Captain's desk in the tiny sweatbox of an office, was a pretty sturdy combination of Hitler, Jack The Ripper and that awful species known as *Tourist, American*. Despicable people.

None of whom he could afford to like very much, warm-hearted, country-proud, woman-loving Italian that he was.

It was a muggy Wednesday in Italy. *Molto humido*, again.

Mercoledi in Roma.

I can't remember a Wednesday so dark as to have hindered the coming Thursday. All my Thursdays. And then some.

You see, the worst part of it all was that Captain Michele Santini was close enough to the truth. Half a truth can be just as damaging as none, sometimes. I was a spy, without portfolio, for the President of the United States, and I was in Italy to do a job for him. Another job which I had considered a piece of cake and no trouble at all. Or rather, less trouble than usual. It says here.

But I hadn't planted bombs and explosives devices all over Rome.

I do believe in Urban Renewal but not that kind.

Yet, I had left Joy Deveau at the Fontana di Trevi on the sultry night of July the twenty third. Left her drinking the coke.

But I hadn't left her dead.

Never dead.

I don't murder sharp gals with quiet, good looks.

I don't murder anybody, unless put upon.

Unless they try to out-draw me.

But that was beside the point, now.

Captain Michele Santini had me by the short hairs.

And my hair is short enough, as it is.

'Well, *Signor?* Have you thought? Have you thought hard? This, as you can readily see, is no small matter. Since the Pietá was almost demolished by that lunatic last year, we have come to appreciate, here in Rome, exactly what we can no longer afford to lose. As for the young lady — we do not like murders, *Signor*. Especially when the victim is a beautiful *signorina* who obviously had so much to live for.'

'I get the message, Captain Santini.' Now it was I who was very weary. And feeling trapped and hemmed in with his cramped office and far-reaching love for mankind. And womankind. And Rome. 'I do, indeed.'

'So. And what is your answer? Or rather, your defence against all these charges?'

'I didn't do it. Any of it. How's that for openers?'

'Not good enough, I am afraid. However, I am a just man, *Signor*. If you care to re-consider your answer — '

'You'll throw the book at me. Is that it?'

'*Si, Signor.*' His bleak smile was slightly malicious. 'And in this case, the book is your oh so convenient diary. Don't you agree? Never has a defendant, in my experience, been so co-operative in that way. To record all the dates, all the places — and even his victim.'

'You're a meanie, Santini, but I read you loud and clear. And now it is you who compel me to make like the average tourist.'

'*Come?*' His frown was beautiful to behold. 'What do you mean?'

I put my teeth together and leaned back in my chair.

'Call the United States Embassy. Before you bury me altogether.'

The good Captain leaned forward in his own chair, pyramiding his fingers, shrugging his shoulders, blinking his eyes.

'You insist?'

'I insist.'

'Then you leave me no alternative, *Signor.*'

'Now, what do *you* mean?'

'There will be no call permitted to your Embassy, you will be held incommunicado and no one, Signor Noon, will be allowed to contact you until you are seen by our people from the Military. Unless, of course, you make a full confession here and now and spare all of us this useless procrastination of yours.'

'See beautiful Rome,' I said bitterly, unable to completely believe what he had said, 'and lose all your rights.'

'Bombers and murderers are animals to us, *Signor*,' Captain Michele Santini rapped in a low snarl. 'Until you can convince me otherwise, you will be treated as such.'

He proved to be as good as his word.

They treated me like a dog.

It was *Mondo Cane* from that moment on.

3

Three Corpses In the Fountain

*'Men's evil manners live in brass;
their virtues We write in Water . . .'*
William Shakespeare

They weren't playing games with me,
either. Neither checkers, dominoes or
Bluffing Poker. I'd lost the trick to
Santini.

The good Captain Michele Santini,
and whoever might be backing up his
official play as to what to do with the
detectivo privato from the great United
States across the waters. Santini rang a
bell, summoned two of his uniformed
strong-arms and I was thrown into the
Roma lock-up without any further to do
or to don't. They escorted me from the
tiny office, down three flights of winding,
wooden stairs, into a stone dungeon of
a cell, windowless, that called down

echoes of the old Bastille in Paris during the Revolution. I went quietly, without kicking up a storm or screaming about my rights because there was far too much to think out. And puzzle over. And get my second wind about. Something was wrong. Very wrong.

And there was nothing to be gained from resistance.

The ball game had already begun and though I knew whose side I was on, I wasn't that sure exactly of the batting order. The President had called the strategy but not even he could have prepared for my possible arrest as a man who planted explosive devices all over the tourist attractions of Rome and as the murderer of a harmless, vacationing teenage girl drowned in the Fontana di Trevi. The Chief could not have bargained for that.

Santini's watchdogs must have counted me an extraordinarily dangerous prisoner. Losing the Colt, attaché case and luggage was one thing but the routine that followed was right out of Murderer's Row in Ossining. They took my shoes, they took my tie, they took the wide leather belt from my waist, confiscated my wrist watch and cocktail ring. And that wasn't all. Whatever the ground rules were of Captain Santini's detaining and confining procedure, they lifted my silver cigarette lighter, personal keys and loose change — literally anything that could be described as a weapon or tool with which to do myself in. I stood still for all of it because the two, burly, six-foot Carabinieri seemed to be just spoiling for me to put up some kind of fight so they could have an excuse to slap me around. I could read between the lines of their sullen, swarthy Romany faces. As a despoiler of their beloved Roma and a butcher of lovely young *signorini*, I deserved nothing but the worst at their avenging hands.

They even stripped me of the *P.O.W.-MIA* silver-plated bracelet which I'd been wearing as my own sort of private protest against the Vietnam War. MAJ. NORLAN DAUGHTREY *8–2–65* didn't cut any ice with the two young cops. They practically sneered when they read the inscription It was obviously too late for peace of any kind.

Peace at any price.

And then they left me, slamming the dungeon door shut, sliding the iron bolt on the outside home into its groove with a thunder like the end of the world. They padlocked the barrier, too, rattling a lot of keys and things. There was a grilled Judas Window in the face of the door, convenient for pushing through trays of food and containers of liquid. It all could have been very laughable, the entire routine, if it wasn't so ominously for real. There wasn't a chair, bed or carpet in the stone room. Just the four cinder-block formation walls, flagstone floor and ceiling and the whole affair was no more than ten feet square. There was no graffiti on the walls, though anything by Edmond Dantes wouldn't have surprised me at all. It was as if the little cubicle was spotlessly clean, just to accommodate me. Whatever air there was trickled in from the outer passageway. Warm, heavy and close. The atmosphere reeked of stale dust, ancient times and the *gabinetto*. I wouldn't have to ask where that was. It couldn't have been more than two yards from my front door.

All in all, my present location in Rome was not exactly a garden spot or even a room at the local *Y*. To say the very least.

I sat down on the stone floor, put my back to the wall and began to think. I thought for a very long time. Kilroy was *not* here.

There was a lot to ponder over.

Regardless of the serious charges, why would a Captain Michele Santini treat a rather celebrated American detective, as if he was less than human? And more than monstrous?

I didn't know.

To get at the possible answers, or maybe just to keep the panic button out of reach, I mentally tried a Questions and Answers game with myself. The sort of give-and-take I hadn't treated Captain Santini to.

Because I couldn't. Without losing the whole ball of wax.

But alone in that tough little cell, with

no Police Steno to put my answers down and into the record, to hang me with, it was an easy thing to do. No sweat at all. Mental therapy, really.

And it kept me from losing my nerve.

Kept me from thinking about the fix I was in.

Signor, why have you come to Roma at this time?

I came because it is my job, Captain Santini.

Your job, *Signor*? Please explain.

I'm on special duty at all times with the President of my country. What you might call his very own special investigator. So special that nobody else but him knows that my job exists. Or that I work in that capacity. You might say, I'm an invisible man.

Ah, I see. A secret agent, eh?

Something like that.

And again I ask — what are you doing in Roma?

You won't believe it, Captain —

Try me. I have heard stranger things than you might think.

Okay. How's this? He sent me here

to pick up some special documents for him from our Embassy. Something he couldn't trust to the ordinary diplomatic courier. Or to any of the mailing and delivery agencies. And before you ask, no, I don't know what the documents are. Or what they could be. In effect, I'm only an errand boy this trip.

Then why does the errand boy come by such a circuitous route? Paris and then to Rapallo before coming directly here?

Window-dressing, strictly. To make it appear as if I was on vacation, living it up. Seeing the Continent. Fun in the Sun. Etcetera.

But why the arsenal then? The guns, the explosives — surely, these documents cannot be so important as all that —

You say. In our kind of work, be prepared is the motto. Boy scout or not. You'd be surprised the opposition you can run into.

Then why did you dawdle while you were here? Making the grand tour of the sights and the exhibits. Or was that more of your window-dressing, as you say, *Signor*?

You catch on quick, Captain. Exactly that. The documents weren't to be ready for my pick-up until yesterday. I was just about to go to the Embassy when your men showed up and changed my plans.

Ah. So you say, *Signor*. And who were you to see at the Embassy? Who was the one who would hand over these documents to you? Surely, not your esteemed Ambassador — ?

I can't tell you that, Captain. No way.

And I can't believe you, Signor Noon. No way, as you say. Yet even if I did — why does a grown man keep a diary? Like some schoolboy? Why is it such a coincidence that you have this arsenal on your person and nearly every place you visited — we find a bomb planted? Tell me that.

It's the way I am. I'm a Romantic, Captain Santini. Rome captivates me. I flip for the big statues, the paintings. Everything. I —

You will forgive me, *Signor*, but I no longer believe anything you say. More than that, the murder of the *Signorina* takes away any sympathy I might have had for you. Even the idiot who tried to destroy the Pietá harmed no one but himself. *Allora*, we will check your story about these documents at the Embassy —

That will get you nothing. I told you. It's all hush-hush. No one will own up to knowing me or my mission. They can't afford to.

Don't tell me what my job is, *Signor*. We will see.

All right. Go ahead. Do your own thing. But would you mind telling me what made you pick me up in the first place?

Of course. The waiter at the restaurant in the *piazza* where the Pantheon stands recalls you talking to the girl at the fountain while you were drinking your *colas* . . .

I didn't hear him say that, naturally, because Captain Santini had never told me how he'd glommed onto me. It was easy enough to imagine the rest of his questions and answers. There was no doubt where he stood in the matter of Ed Noon *vs*. Roma. Tourists would always come out second in his book. Especially ones who kept diaries to record their foul deeds. And if I had confessed to him the true nature of my presence in Rome, the liaison man between the White House and the U.S. Embassy on the Via Veneto, he would have scoffed all night.

Which left me exactly nowhere.

Or rather squatting on my rusty dusty in Santini's jailhouse, wondering what to do next. Wondering who was trying to blow up Rome, who killed Joy Deveau and what precisely was the reality of the all-important documents I was to pick up from a man called Flood who was connected in some way with the staff of the Embassy. The Chief had never told me. Not really. He never spells it all out.

All of which left me in great shape.

I didn't even know what time it was now, thanks to Santini's little helpers. And if he was lining me up for a Military Tribunal of some kind, I was in hotter water than there is in a cheap boiler.

There was no way I could contact the Chief and radio an *SOS*.

That was strictly against the rules of the game. No *May Days*.

I was on my own. Because it had to be that way.

I'd have to bail the ship out, all alone.

With or without paddles, oars and .45.

When I caught myself staring at the flagstone ceiling, silently clocking the slow scuttle of a huge black water bug jogging over to the next wall and thinking the insect was making better time than I was, I stopped playing mental quiz games with the absent Captain Michele Santini. The demoralising effects of imprisonment, any kind, of any duration, had slyly gulled me into an inactive state. I recognised the familiar symptoms. I was feeling sorry for myself. Wishing could not get me out of Santini's durance vile. Only constructive thinking would. Nothing else works. Stone walls do not a prison make or iron bars a cage, maybe — but unless I got cracking, Santini's cell would ruin me.

I stood up, took a military position and went into about twenty knee bends, like training for the Olympics. Then I dropped down, extended my legs, put my heels together and did twenty push-ups. To top off all that stimulating put-the-blood-back-into-your veins exertion, I tried some Karate moves, adding the vocal grunts and plosives to give it some genuine juice. Maybe it all didn't make too much sense, but after ten minutes of intensive gymnastics, I was ready to go about five rounds with Santini's burly six-footers.

It cleared my head, too.

Driving out the cobwebs, the confusion, the mild fear.

And I knew that Santini didn't have a damn thing on me. No proof, no clues, no evidence. Except possibly the small annoyance that I carried a working arsenal with me in my travels.

There was nothing to link me with the planted explosive devices. Rome had millions of tourists every year.

With or without bombs. *PI* cards and attaché cases.

44

And there wasn't a scrap of anything to connect me with Joy Deveau, a teenage wanderer I'd only met once and hardly knew.

Nor could Santini ever possibly tie me into the U.S. Embassy and my secret mission for the President of the United States.

But — he must have had something to move in on me so fast and so sure of himself. So sure of his case. So unafraid of consequences.

About *that*, you can never know.

Not until they tell you.

I had to wonder when Captain Michele Santini would.

In the meantime, I wasn't enjoying his hospitality at all.

As hot as the day had been, the cell got colder as Time crept on. The square stone room grew tomb-like. There was no sound of life, the bells of the city couldn't be heard and no one came to gloat or feed me. I could feel my unshaved face growing hair.

But the worst thing going was I didn't even have a cigarette to comfort myself with. They had taken those from me, too.

I tried not to chew my nails as I waited.

It wasn't easy not to.

For a Nicotine Nick like me, it was the toughest torture of all.

No smokes.

I lost all track of Time.

★ ★ ★

When the dungeon door rattled and the iron bolt growled in its groove, I snapped erect as if suddenly, ice water had been sloshed all over me. The effect was that startling. What little light that was left in the windowless room, fed in from the illuminated passageway, had become no more than dim slivers of pale amber cast-offs from a bulb of some kind. I blinked like a stupid owl. For two reasons. To adjust to the change in lighting and because I had been dosing off, sitting with my back to the rear wall, head resting in the cradle of my arms and knees. Boredom and the long wait had taken their toll.

46

The cell was damper and chillier now but that was small potatoes compared to the ominous and deathly silent group crowding into the room. I sprang erect, frightened game surrounded by hunters. I backed up to the wall, in boxing position, fighting to see what was going on. My flashing view of the new world thrust upon me was about three uniforms, helmeted heads, dark shadows stretching higher than my own six feet. My brain churned and my heart flip-flopped. Like I had told Captain Santini, I knew very little about foreign police procedure. My terrified imagination put truncheons and axes in the hands of the three shadows converging on me. And worse.

I'd been in stationhouses before. Lots of times. But this nightmare was something novel, even for me. Right out Nazi Germany and *1984*. And the Dark Ages. I nearly lost my head.

But the dungeon door did not slam shut and a broad swathe of full yellow illumination flooded the stone room. The uniformed trio fanned out, as if stepping back, and one of the shadows suddenly laughed in a very harsh, yet musically Italian voice.

'*Madonna* — the face you put on, *Signor*! Did you think we had come to work you over, eh? Your *Americano* third degree?'

'*Brutta faccia*,' hissed a shadow close by. 'How a face can look so ugly when the man is frightened!'

'*Basta, basta!*' The third gentle soul in uniform snapped out peevish words. 'Enough of this. Give him back his belongings and get him out of here. Bad enough we have to do Santini's dirty work for him. Let us not prolong the situation, my friends.'

I could only stare at them, without being able to see their faces very clearly, for their backs were still to the hallway light. Brain, heart and mind slowed down to a slow-motion, floating sensation. Almost a stop-freeze action sequence. Or just a silent movie.

'*What the hell is this?*'

There was no way of recognising the hoarse, cracked whisper as my own. And everything was going much too fast, now.

For they were giving me back my tie and belt. The watch, the shoes, the cigarette lighter and pack of Camels, the cocktail ring, the *P.O.W.-MIA* silver-plated bracelet, the keys and loose change. Everything I had walked in with, including my freedom. The brown diary was handed over, too. Fumbling dumbly, I dropped it, still blinking foolishly like that dull old owl rousted from his sleep in the barn. I had to be dreaming in the middle of the Roma night.

Something was way off base. Out of kilter. Out of sync.

Something was.

Patiently, slightly more cordially and perhaps even a trifle generously, one of the three shadows, explained what had happened.

' — we ask your pardon, *Signor*. A regrettable mistake. Our good *capitano* begs you to understand and to forgive. You see, there have been two other ladies found in the water since your arrest. The coroner is most certain about the times of death. Therefore, it could not possibly have been yourself who committed these terrible calamities. As for the business of explosive devices, the Vatican has relayed to us the confidential information that they are satisfied with your identity — it seems you are highly regarded by Papa Paul himself! Therefore, it also follows you would not be the sort of fellow to bomb our beloved attractions. In a word, *Dio!* — the Pope is recommendation enough for an army, let alone one *Americano*. Further, the Vatican Security boys tell us they are well on the trail of those who may be responsible for these things. A terrorist group from the North country who call themselves *The Arcangeli* — but come, *Signor*. Finish your dressing and we will see to your comforts. Dinner, a bottle of *vino*, eh?, and perhaps even a *bella ragazza* to make up for this terrible inconvenience to yourself. We do humbly beg your pardon — *prego*.'

'*Prego*,' I echoed dully. Trying to dress, trying to think.

There was a definite stink of something in the cold little cell.

And it didn't come from the *gabinetto*

nearby, wherever it was.

Not even the tremendous relief of No Third Degree or Worse, could quite dissolve the ineluctable conclusion that all was not too right with the world. Especially the Rome universe.

Three women were dead. Murdered, to hear the Carabinieri tell it.

There were bombs popping up like daisies all over the historic landscape. The Eternal City was practically mined. Another Normandy.

And I still hadn't picked up the package from the Embassy.

And Santini had hauled me into the net only to turn me loose.

Somehow, it was all jumbled and tricky like Chinese boxes.

Like a kaleidoscope off-centre.

Out of focus. Distorted. A maze of odds and evens.

I dressed quietly, ignoring the three helmeted shadows standing by, ready to wait on me hand and foot. Courteously, penitently, but still richly amused by the spectacle of the terror I had shown. It may have been their own private sport with the average tourist who committed a felony or a misdemeanor. I couldn't be sure.

Sort of a Roman oneupmanship.

All I was sure of was that I despised them from helmet to booted heel. I can't stand terrorists of any kind. Never mind *The Arcangeli*.

They must have sensed my lack of love, my three shadows.

They didn't return my .45 and shoulder harness and ammo clip. Not until we were upstairs on the floor outside of Santini's office and it seemed I might have cooled down some. I kept a tight smile on my face, indicating no hard feelings, but inside I was Vesuvius. The label — *cop* — Italian style — had taken on a new, very personal meaning. I felt like a bewildered, angry young man on the campus at Kent University. Wanting to smash and break official faces.

'Come,' one of the shadows chuckled jovially. 'Show there are no bad feelings, eh? Have a glass of Chianti with us — '

'Thanks, no. Mustn't drink. Doctor's orders.'

'Then let us take you to meet Silvana,' begged a second shadow. 'Big, breasts like *mezza-melone*! We make use of her from time to time in our work. You will devour her. She is a feast of a woman! *Bellissiima*. You like them dark, yes?'

'She can't be the Silvana I have in mind. But don't worry about me. I've got distribution of my own. Diners Club card and everything.'

'You are a strange *tourista* indeed, Signor Noon.' The third shadow speaking was the one who had been Santini's apologiser. 'Most men come to Rome only for the drinking and our women — '

'I'm queer for museums. And statues.' I stared at the three of them very hard. They were no longer shadows, of course. The light in the long hall was really very good. They were all tall, wide-shouldered and young. Bronzed, white-toothed and silkily masculine. So many Vittorio Gassmans. Dames would drool over them, more or less. 'What about my luggage?' I was holding the brown diary like a Bible, now.

'It has all been returned to the hotel.

Cento dieci Via Nomentana. All in order. Captain Santini was most explicit. You have your precious arsenal intact, *Signor*. There will be no further trouble. I, Hugo, promise you that. It is the least we can do, eh?'

'Fair enough, Hugo. And these are — ?' I gestured to his two compatriots. They beamed at me but they were still smirking. Slyly.

'Alfredo and Gino,' Hugo purred. 'My comrades-in-arms.'

'Hugo, Alfredo and Gino,' I repeated, tasting the names. 'I'll remember that. Never know when I might need a policeman again. By the way — what is the Italian word for *pig*?'

'*Porco*,' Hugo answered readily enough but there was a guarded, quizzical expression in his eyes. 'And why do you ask, *Signor*?'

'Just wanted to keep all the labels in place.' I moved away from them, heading toward the front door of the stationhouse and the lovely outside air. 'Well, I won't say godbye, gentlemen. We will meet again. I'm sure of it. *Arrivederci*.'

They watched me go, alternately shaking their heads, amused to a man and completely missing the flat, atonal pronunciation I gave the word of farewell. I had delivered it with all the twangy resonance of a first-week Italian Language scholar. Or a Midwestern tourist.

I took my leave of Santini's Carabinieri. Hugo, Alfredo and Gino. Three little pigs in fancy uniforms and phony *simpatico*.

They didn't give a damn what happened to me. They never would.

I walked out into the dark Roma night, looking for bigger and more important game.

The wolf.

The Big Bad Wolf. Who is international and speaks all languages.

A He-Wolf or a She-Wolf. Perhaps, even both.

The one who possibly had engineered a false arrest and a time-consuming detention while He or She finagled around at the United States Embassy trying to foul up the assignment which had brought me to Europe. A top secret Presidential mission.

There seemed to be no other logical explanation for Captain Michele Santini's incredible performance of his official duty.

Maybe there was a girl-murderer who left corpses in the water fountains of Rome, maybe there was a mad bomber, maybe there was an *Arcangeli* terrorist group but it made no sense at all that I should be arrested in the first place and then treated like a desperate character in an Iron Curtain country, in the second.

And then, even more unbelievably, let go so easily.

My copper's nostrils were curling mightily. The vibes were all wrong. Especially for an operative in my particular line of work.

Rome glowed, showing a million fireflies of illumination, as I hit the street. Descending the low stone staircase to the sidewalk.

The Eternal City lay under a blanket of heat and humidity.

Waiting like a streetwalker greeting her next customer.

Gaudily, hotly, damply — the *compleat*

whore. Wanton and wide open.

With a lot of surprises and shocks between her fleshy and vulgar thighs. From the heights of the Palantine to the depths of the Fontana di Trevi. From the top of the Spanish Steps to Bernini's tub.

Death also waited in Rome that night.

Like a whore, Death also services everyone.

Who can make the price.

None of us are ever out of pocket when it comes to that.

We're all rich enough to die.

And nobody can live forever.

Not lately.

Not any place in the world.

4

The Seven Kills Of Rome

'When in Rome, do as the Romans do.'

— Anonymous.

Nobody was waiting up for me at the Villa del Parco. Nobody was hanging around the oblong, faintly motel-model lobby which overlooked a sloping driveway, bordered with grass, feeding down to the main thoroughfare. The Via Nomentana was a comparatively isolated stretch of asphalt, free of casual strollers and heavy traffic. At nine in the evening, it was practically Horace Harding Boulevard on Long Island. The Rome face was masked. Whatever guests the hotel owned, were either all in bed or out somewhere doing the *La Dolce Vita* routine. I couldn't have cared less. There was too much to do before midnight.

A new man at the panelled front desk favoured me with an expressionless stare as I came up the drive into the lobby. A fast glance at the pigeon-holed rack behind him showed no mail or messages or calls for *Camera Numero Vingt-Cinque*. Room Number Twenty Five was mine. And the new desk man hadn't been on duty when Captain Santini's flying squad had descended on me earlier in the day. His bored attitude gave him away.

When I asked him for the room key, he went all owl on me, comically. Blinking his eyes rapidly, tightening his mouth like the spring on a cheap watch and pulling his hand back as if I had leprosy. I showed him my teeth, said nothing and marched across the lobby, disappearing behind the door of the tiny foyer which led to Room Twenty Five. I was sure his eyes drilled holes into my back the full distance. There was no blaming him, really. Rome couldn't have been the most exciting place in the world to a homegrown Italian. Especially on one more *molto humido* day.

Locking the door of the room, I got organised in a hurry.

The luggage and attaché case were neatly placed on the floor between the white cane chair and the cedarwood bureau. Checking them took only a few careful minutes. Everything seemed to be as before. Santini had kept his promise. I was still the owner of plastic explosives, gimmicked pistol-lighters, ammunition and assorted James Bond weapons. Again, it was surprising that the Captain should be so charitable, whether I was authorised or not. Licensed or not.

Nothing had been touched or re-arranged.

Everything looked to be in working order.

Frowning, I placed the thick brown leather diary among my shirts and socks in the suitcase. My diary-keeping days were over. As far as Rome was concerned. Writing wasn't going to solve things.

Food was no longer a problem because I had stopped en route from the lock-up to stoke down a ham and cheese sandwich and two cups of American coffee in a sidewalk restaurant near the Piazza del Popolo.

Sitting there in the muggy night, staring up at the lovely obelisk in the centre of the setting, had calmed me down considerably after the farce with Hugo, Alfredo and Gino. The moon was a white balloon and it wasn't saying *Yankee, Go Home*!

But now I was thirsty. Drier than Utah at high noon.

The little refrigerator in the corner of the room, provided by the Villa del Parco for all its patrons, was a never-empty store of soft drinks, beer, wines and sundry other goodies. I found a small bottle of *aranciata* and took care of Utah. *Aranciata* is nothing more than orange pop but it helped kill the heat. There was no point in hitting the joy juice just yet. A big night loomed ahead. I had to be on my toes to beat somebody to the punch. Somebody with curious ideas about Embassy documents and errand boys.

I lit a Camel, thought very carefully for about five minutes, and reached the only conclusion possible. Time was a crucial factor, now, and there wasn't very much of it left. Mission-Time, that is.

I got comfortable on the slightly lumpy bed and picked up the phone. Wherever you may wander, telephones look and operate pretty much alike. And they serve the very same purpose, too.

'*Prego?*' said the man on the desk out there in the lobby. He no longer sounded bored. Just eager and slightly nervous.

'Could you get me an outside number, please?'

'*Sí*. As you wish, *Signor. Numero* — ?'

I gave him the special listing I had been given by the President for the American Embassy building on the Via Veneto. One that was not printed in the directory of Rome. Despite the hour, the line could not be busy. The party known as Flood was expecting to hear from me.

Twenty four hours had gone by. Far beyond the planned rendezvous time but that shouldn't matter, anymore. Someone was supposed to be waiting. Flood, specifically. He couldn't move without me.

The Roma Telephone Company was miles behind Bell. There were about fourteen clicks and twenty one buzzes of electrical sound and Room Twenty Five was getting hotter, when someone in that mysterious U.S. Embassy Building on the Via Veneto finally got on the line.

'Yes. Who's calling, please?'

The voice was guarded, unaccented. Male. A voice that might belong to an unctuous librarian or a self-satisfied bank manager.

'In nineteen hundred and twenty nine,' I declared, 'Mel Ott of the New York Giants batted three forty nine, hit forty two home runs and drove in one hundred and fifty one baserunners.'

A strangled sound, half snarl and half surprise, spluttered and died. When the voice came back, it had steely control of itself.

'And how old was he when he accomplished all this?'

'Twenty. They don't hardly make them that way anymore. He was The Little Giant.'

'So it would seem. And who won

the Academy Award for Best Actress in nineteen hundred and fifty four?' The pre-arranged code was working.

'Grace Kelly. And I didn't believe it for a second.'

'*Great God Almighty!*' the placid voice exploded, all pretence put aside. '*Where the hell have you been, Mister Noon?*'

'You wouldn't believe that, either. I'll tell you when I see you. I'm going to see you, Mr. Flood. Aren't I?'

'Yes, you're going to see me! These damn papers are bringing me to the brink of perdition! Man, do you realise how important this matter is — ' Flood was amazing me. You'd expect a diplomat or whatever the hell he was to have more poise going for him. But then again, maybe he was new at real Cloak-and-Dagger games. 'Oh, I've heard of you, Mr. Noon. And your reputation for success. You like doing things your own way. You're always given your head. But if this is an example of your recklessness, I'll be damned if I know why the Chief — '

'Don't lecture me, Flood. He doesn't and you can't. Just tell me where and when, huh?'

He caught hold of whatever cool he might own and a deep sigh floated over the wire. When he spoke again, a great relief rather than an almost feminine pique filled his tone.

'You're right. Spilled milk is spilled milk, isn't it? Do you know where the Spanish Steps are?'

'Sure. Bernini's Tub at the bottom and the Trinitá dei Monti at the top. The Tub is cracked and filthy but the church is beautiful. And now the Steps are a regular Hippie Heaven. Last time I looked.'

'Good. You're climbing in my estimation already. It is now roughly nine twenty eight. Could you be there at exactly ten thirty?'

'No sweat. It's only twenty minutes from the hotel. Do we meet on the Steps?'

'No. Far too risky. Let's say I'll be at the front door of the church itself. Right behind the obelisk. There's very little street light up there. That can be cover enough — '

'You *will* have the documents with you?'

'Yes.' Flood grew very officious on me, now. 'With your further instructions. Of which I know nothing. You have a black attaché case, according to the file I was given on you. Bring it along. When we meet, we will exchange cases. Mine will contain what you came for. Don't speak to me at all. We'll work out the transfer depending on the layout when we arrive there. Understood?'

'Understood. I know what you look like, Mr. Flood. They ran some movie film for me before I left D.C. But just to play this safe, what can you do to certify that you're the man I'm having this nice chat with? Standard Operating Procedure, old boy.'

He thought about that, taking a healthy pause.

'This line is scrambled, of course. But that's good thinking. Very well. I'll unbutton my coat — it has four buttons and is a dark blue, raglan-sleeve

66

topper — and then I'll re-button it again. Now, what can you do to set my mind at ease? There are so many damn doubles in this infernal business.'

'I'll whistle the first five bars of *You're The Top*. Over and over again. You up on your Cole Porter, Mr. Flood?'

'You're not funny,' he suddenly erupted all over again. Bristling like a porcupine interrupted while eating. 'Really, Mr. Noon, this is a very serious piece of government business all around. I wish you'd stop romanticising. If you would only realise — '

'Another lecture? Okay. No more clowning. Do you know anything at all about three women being murdered — their bodies left in water fountains? Or anything about bombs being planted all over Rome?'

'For God's sake, man! What are you talking about now? If this is another example of your flip, sarcastic — '

'Ten thirty, Flood,' I said, cutting him off for his astounded reaction had told me that he didn't know what I was talking about. 'Sharp. See you then. Start practising on your buttons.'

I hung up on him while he was still making strangling noises.

For men like him, men like me are always pretty hard to take.

With the phone replaced in its black bed, there was nothing more to puzzle over. Contact had been made. The time schedule was way off but Mr. Flood still seemed to be in possession of the Top Secret documents. Captain Santini's routine and the attendant delay didn't seem to have brought any cockroaches out of the woodwork. It was all very strange, didn't make sense and maybe I was off in my diagnosis of the situation but the set-up was still solvent. I had expected practically anything and everything when I phoned the Embassy but there it was. The Status was still Quo. Three drowned and murdered dolls and explosive devices suddenly didn't seem to have a blessed thing to do with what had brought me to Rome.

There was little else to do except meet Flood, pick up the new black attaché case and go back home to the White House with the goods.

It all looked so easy at nine thirty five, Roma Time.

Those could have been Very Famous Last Words.

What was waiting for Flood and I on the darkened Spanish Steps at ten thirty defies description. Or explanation.

And analysis.

And belief.

I was walking into a slaughterhouse and I didn't know it.

With my eyes wide open.

And screaming.

Seven people would be dead before the clock in the stone face of the *Trinitá dei Monti* struck eleven.

Seven.

Count them.

Seven!

And no less than six of them would be innocent bystanders.

Great God Almighty.

To quote Mr. Flood.

5

Slaughter On the Spanish Steps

'He made the trains run on time.'
Tribute to Benito Mussolini.

Hot darkness hung over the Monumental Steps like a changeless weather forecast. The Steps had only been there since 1722 but Time, uncounted millions of people — tourists, natives and what-have-you — had left no footprints on the great stone stairway. There were three climbing tiers of wide, sprawling stairs, bordered on each side by banks of July flowers, wildly coloured, scented and mainly crimson. Seen in the Roman night, enveloped in blankets of muggy warmth, crowded with hordes of idlers, lovers and Hippies all waiting for their next check from home — an American Express office right down the block from Bernini's water fountain did a gold-rush business — the Spanish

70

Steps rose proudly, with a traditional kind of implacable serenity, untouched by the advance of Civilisation. The Bomb, Vietnam, Civil Rights and Cancer cut no ice here. None at all. The pound could devaluate, the *lira* crumble but the Steps would be there forever. Guitarists filled the close night with four-four rhythms, teenage couples giggled and did their own thing, the Old Ones tottered by, out of the mainstream if anybody asked them but alive and part of the picturesque setting just the same. The round Italian moon was a half-baked pizza riding overhead. Beaming down romantically.

I marched up the darkened stairs, heading for the two small matching gardens filled with mountains of more flowers. Right above their florally-rich patterns, the towering stone obelisk stood eternal guard duty squarely before the massive double doors of the Trinitá dei Monti. The twin cupolas of the old church rose upward into the sky. Twin turrets atop a feudal castle. The black attaché case tucked under my right arm would have fooled anybody. It wasn't empty because it was now stuffed with two editions of the daily periodicals to lend an aura of some weight. There was no telling what might come up. Flood's agenda for the evening could need some fast improvising. In any case, there was nothing and no one else to think about as I moved up the Spanish Steps. Not even the Keats-Shelley Room down below which was closed until the morning. Vera Cacciatore had gone home.

Unisex Hippies, girls and boys lost in the usual costumes of long hair, jeans, love beads and peace necklaces, had used each tier of the stairway to set up sidewalk businesses, huckstering curios, artwork and oddments in the charms and notions line, to feather their Roman nests with whatever scratch the traffic would bear. *La Dolce Vita* danced on but it always needs some money to make it work at all. I ignored everybody, hardly looking to the left or the right. The time was uncomfortably close to ten thirty. Another *autista*, a possible reject from the *Mille Miglia*, had whipped me from the Villa del Parco, stopping directly alongside Bernini's Tub at the base of the Steps in fantastically breath-taking minutes. The stair climb took almost five minutes more. It was literally jammed with humanity.

Suddenly, I was over the top, the stairs behind me, the impressive façade of the Trinitá dei Monti, a healthy spit away. Flood was right. A solitary street lamp seemed to be all that illuminated the area. The curving, cobbled street, bending crookedly off to the centre of town, leading toward the very middle of the celebrated Via Veneto, was like a dark and menacing alleyway. Without the full moon, the church environs would have been blacker than a bishop's cassock. Visibility was poor, as it was.

There was no sign of Mr. Flood of the United States Embassy.

There was nobody near the front doors of the church.

There was only a white ice cream truck, garishly emblazoned with painted facsimiles of its wares. A gaggle of six people flocked around the vehicle, pushing and clamouring for ices, *gelati, aranciata* and *cola*, to kill the thirst brought on by the after-sundown humidity. I elbowed around the mob, stepping across the tarred street toward the front stairway leading into the Trinitá dei Moni. The gigantic stone obelisk dwarfed us all. Like a great stone finger pointing skyward.

It didn't seem to be a night for Religion, either. The church front was serenely desolate and untouched. Of course, there might be a packed house inside. I couldn't know otherwise unless I went in. I only knew that nobody was going in. That Mr. Flood was late for the appointment. That God was unwanted that night.

He must have known something nobody else did.

The way things turned out.

The small city that is Rome, built on seven hills, was ready for another piece of gory history. Not unlike the Colosseum variety of A.D. when Constantine was trying on his first pair of Emperor sandals. And trying to talk his bloodthirsty fellow Roman citizens out of human carnival doings in the huge old stadium-amphitheatre-circus. The Arena, with all its brutal Games. The Nero kicks.

My .45 was riding high in its shoulder harness. The black leather attaché case itched strangely in my fingers. I peered all around the half-lit darkness surrounding the Trinitá dei Monti, on the lookout for Mr. Flood. The ice cream truck customers filled the night with cries and murmurs of glee, impatience and just plain exuberance in equal parts. No tourists, they. Their collective uproar was pure Italian. With all the stops out. Lusty and loud.

Overhead, the round church clock, set in the left tower below one of the twin cupolas, showed a disappointing *ten forty five*. Flood wasn't only late. He was dangerously over-due for a man with an imperative, undercover mission. I tried not to worry, standing in the shadowy recesses of he church's angled stone stairway, leading up to the front doors. But it was a sweat, all the same. Secret operators should always keep their rendezvous on schedule.

Minutes flew by, each one worth a drop of perspiration and fear.

And then, on the verge of some kind of decision, one way or the other, I saw him. Saw him the way I didn't want to see him.

Quick. All in a flash, like a magic trick. A conjuring act.

With a stunning burst of realisation. And wonder.

He was running.

Running for his life.

Toward the church, toward me, burgeoning out of that yawning darkness of the side street winding downward to the Via Veneto.

There was no need to whistle *You're The Top*, anymore.

He was wearing a dark blue, four-button, raglan sleeve topper, all right, but he was strangely hatless and the bald gleam of his round skull bobbing atop a tall, angular body, as he swept under the solitary street light, was a shining blur of trouble. His face was a rictus of agony. Either from the exertions of a very long run or something else I couldn't see. I never did find out. All at once, the whole scene, the set-piece, the tableau, was that ancient, achingly familiar one of *Oh, Oh! Something's gone wrong!*

The awesome signs were unmistakable.

Diplomats don't have to run. And Mr. Flood was galloping.

The black attaché case swinging from his flapping arm was a duplicate of the one I held. And the pounding tattoo of Flood's shoes slapping the paved sidewalk, as narrow as the lane was, echoed like the drumbeats of doom. In a furious medley of leather and stone.

He spotted me within flying seconds, his open-mouthed face closing in a fast smile that would have warmed my heart under the other circumstances. He looked like a pilgrim seeing Christ. With a gasp of breath, he re-doubled his efforts and plunged on toward me. From more than thirty feet away. I sprang down from the church steps to meet him, going for the hardware under my left armpit. The Colt .45.

Suddenly, the Roman night was alive with terror.

And other sounds besides Flood's thundering footfalls and the gabbling chorus of customers across the small areaway in front of the Trinitá dei Monti.

Flood, racing and lurching toward me, shouted something.

It was a warning, a cry for help and a plea. All in one blurting expulsion of vocal force. The .45 jumped into my hand as I bridged the distance between myself and Flood.

Almost, that is. I never did get to him in time.

The miss was worse than the proverbial mile. A disaster.

When I saw the woman, it was too late to do anything about her. Or change things. Like Mr. Flood, she loomed like an apparition from somewhere behind the hurtling figure of the man from the Embassy, out of the darkness like a monster in a bad dream. A ghoul.

Everything that followed her materialisation happened with such meteoric speed that the flashing image of a tall woman with very long dark hair, dressed in a flowing trenchcoat tightly belted about the middle, evaporated with the deafening explosions of bursting orange and blue flame erupting within the close confines of the very summit of the Spanish Steps and the base of the historic old church.

There was nothing but Death, after that.

And not a single chance for me to get in a shot to stop the slaughter or alter the outcome. I could have been a marble Moses.

The woman in the trenchcoat had a machine gun of some kind.

She opened up with the staggering speed of the fastest typewriter in the universe. An expert of terrible ability.

And far more deadly than her efficiency, the tiny clamouring mob of ice cream truck patrons, all lost their heads in one startling, ill-timed choice of movement. In a rush, a concert of flight. In the wrong direction. *Toward* the bursting orange and blue explosions.

Instead of taking cover behind the ice cream truck or running back toward the stairs, only paces away, they all scattered and milled about, disorganised and terrified. Literally rushing into the withering, chattering salvo of automatic fire lighting up the dark night.

Flood got it first.

Nobody should ever have to die that way.

There could have been something comical about the way his tall, gangling body was suddenly checked in mid-air, then hammered and rocked, as if he was trying a frenzied new dance, but there was nothing funny in watching him hit the hard pavement. A hail of lead had cross-stitched his exposed back, slamming him mercilessly into a blinding oblivion. The black attaché case flew from his swinging arm, sailing out of sight. The bald, hatless skull seemed to wash over with torrents of crimson as leaping gouts of blood geysered from his mouth. I jockeyed crazily for position, hoping to snap off a quick shot to kill the woman but I was later than the end of the Vietnam War. The six screaming, panicking citizens of Roma had fatally road-blocked me, running, scrambling, racing pell-mell into the sound and sight of the machine gun. Putting their innocent flesh between myself and the woman in the darkness of the street scene.

The six natives went down like the rice is reaped.

Bleeding, dying. With bubbling, moaning, screeching whimpers and protests of agony. Broken and destroyed beyond repair by a lethal onslaught of machine gun bullets. I'll never get the awful blasting of that murderous chopper out of my brain. Not ever. And there wasn't a single damn thing I could do to halt the carnage. The woman might have been a ruthless Nazi exterminating a sextette of helpless Jews.

They dropped before me. So many lifeless people. Like rag dolls which had never had the gift of Life. Toppling all in a row.

It couldn't have taken more than ten seconds by the clock in the church tower, for all of it to happen. To come to pass.

No longer than that to slaughter seven human beings.

Seven statistics.

One maybe-spy and six innocent bystanders.

But in that frozen, unreal segment of Time, the world rotated madly on its invisible axis and I lost what little was left of the mind you are supposed to bring into espionage work.

I blew my cool. And my head went with it. Along with Reason.

I vaulted over the dead and the dying, cursing, shouting, gun up and firing. Punching maddened shots into the darkness beyond the street lamp. .45 calibre ammo roared and whined, smacking stone, ricochetting savagely into the night. I never heard the pattering feet that had to be running away. I never caught sight of the woman at all. She was gone, blended with all that darkness, disappearing as magically as she had come. Like the girl-monster-ghoul that she had to be.

All about me, blasted bodies lay, crumpled, contorted, bloody. The shattered corpse of Flood, thoroughly butchered on the very stone threshold of the Trinitá dei Monti was a sight to take to the grave. And all the dead were strangers. Except Mr. Flood, in some nebulous, intangible way. We had been partners, if only for brief minutes, in a secret project that might mean a great deal to our country.

Right or wrong. If Stephen Decatur knew what he toasted.

And now, I was the only one still on my feet in a field of Death. The only survivor at *ten fifty one*, Trinitá dei Monti time.

Shock made me incapable of moving. Going after the killer.

I had no memory of cutting loose with the full clip of the .45. My hand was still nervelessly glued to the hot butt. Shaking.

There was no sign of the black leather attaché case which Mr. Flood had brought with him. And it could have contained nothing.

Not that I looked for it.

Beyond a dazed glance at the sidewalk before the church.

The big rounded pizza moon was

still lighting up the ceiling of Roma sky. Clusters of stars had come out. Twinkling brilliantly.

And behind me, I could hear a crying voice, a man's, murmuring over and over in a dazed voice, '*Jesu Cristo . . . Jesu Cristo . . .* ' The owner of the ice cream truck had tagged the slaughter for all time. I couldn't have agreed with him more. God was nowhere in sight.

Now, came the shouting, the hoarse cries of fear, anger and astonishment and somewhere a dog was barking insanely. The night had re-affirmed its status again, with a tumultuous concert of human din and activity. The kind of night music that always attends the stench and spectacle of calamity and catastrophe. And Fear.

Flood was dead. The Spanish Steps cried out in horror.

The attaché case was gone.

Six people had died needlessly.

If you didn't count Mr. Flood.

I had walked into the heart of another nightmare.

There didn't seem to be anything I could do about walking out of it. I was smack in the middle. Involved and caught. Hung up.

And now I was worse off than I had been when Captain Michele Santini had had me under lock and key. Whatever his motives were.

The Roman Holiday had turned into a blood bath.

There was no way at all for me to throw in the towel.

No way.

I was left holding the bag, too.

An attaché case filled with folded newspapers.

I felt like ten kinds of an idiot. *Imbecile*, as they say in Roma. *Molto stupido* and plain damn worthless.

Ed Noon.

Have Gun. Will Travel.

Italy was kicking hell out of my reputation.

What was left of it in the Roman moonlight atop the Spanish Steps near the front doors of The Trinitá dei Monti.

There was only one thing that was for sure. Damn sure.

I wasn't going to hang around waiting

for Captain Michele Santini. And his Carabinieri sweethearts.

Hugo, Alfredo and Gino. The three fuzzy little pigs.

Or anybody else wearing a policeman's uniform.

I took off.

Like a big-assed bird. I would have flown if I could.

Down that darkened side street, running like hell.

Toward the Via Veneto.

The way Flood had come, before he died. And the woman who killed.

I left the tumult and the shouting, and the horror, behind me.

Where it belonged.

6

Violently On the Via Veneto

' . . . *vesta la giubba!!!* . . . '
Caruso singing Pagliacci.

The insane gunfight at the top of the
Piazza di Spagna, no more than a half
hour old and only blocks away, hadn't
seemed to reach the Via Veneto. Those
last two blocks of sidewalk, ending where
the Borghese Gardens spreads out into a
yawning expanse of green Central Park
proportions, were doing business as usual.
All the cane chairs and gaudy umbrellas,
lined up in orderly rows on both sides of
the famous avenue, under which sat the
jaded natives and tourists, might have
been frozen into a still life that would
never change. The Cafe de Paris was
humming, Doney's across the street was
alive and well and doing a land office
trade. The fleet of dark Fiats ready on a

moving line just around the corner, was in constant motion. The sharpshooters, the taxicab drivers of Roma, were enjoying a brisk evening. The full moon, the balmy late night air, the shank of the day, had all combined to make it a typical Via Veneto scene.

The murderous shoot-out, slaughtering seven people, might have been only the sound of fire-crackers going off, back there about ten forty five. It was a mad, mad, mad, mad world. I found an empty table under one of the big umbrellas in front of the Cafe de Paris, nailed a waiter in dress clothes with black tie and ordered American coffee and a dry Martini. The waiter resembled a dyspeptic Gregory Peck whose reptilian gaze swept over me without comment of any kind. I didn't bother wondering what he could make of a rather breathless *Americano*, carrying a black leather attaché case long after office hours, who also looked as if he had just come off a mad dash to the border. I needed that java and firewater real bad. My table was squeezed between two others, both of which held reasonable facsimiles of the local night life. Fellini could have cast them. The table on my left was queened over by a sleek, ageing, still-attractive brunette in expensive culottes and blooming picture hat, studiously turning the pages of *Paris Match*, as if she was considering posing for the cover or buying a thousand shares of its stock. On my right sat a young Romeo with the requisite white teeth, shining black kinky curls and full Mod suit with thick canary yellow tie, who was wrapped in sexy conclave with a nymphet model whose spilling corn-blonde hair and ample dimensions, freely showing in a tight, crimson miniskirt, would have shocked anybody's Aunt Fanny. Their voices were low, unhurried and reeking with boudoir overtures. The sleek creation reading *Paris Match* couldn't have cared less. Neither could I. The tables all down the line were overflowing with people of all nations. There were saris, turbans, Rotary pins, uniforms, beards, spectacles, evening clothes, furs, glittering jewellery — a dozen accents — the works.

Si, oui, da, ja and you said it, old man.

When the coffee and Martini came, I ordered them all over again, the waiter raised his eyebrows, shrugged, and I dutifully began to nibble on the gin special. I had to think. And think fast.

The black leather attaché case, filled with newspapers, lay in plain sight atop the round table. I stared at it, wanting it to help me think. Objects, the cause of it all, can help sometimes.

Diagonally from the Cafe de Paris, across the street and barely a block away, the darkened mass of the United States Embassy building loomed in the night, just at the crest of the hill before the setting dropped down toward the base of the curving thoroughfare where another fountain by Bernini ruled the roost. The Fountain of the Triton. Rome and its water fountains. You could go off your rocker trying to count them. Regardless of what all the tourist guides said, you could never hear them either.

The roar and zoom of the Fiat and the motorcycle had reduced Roma to the familiar status of Mad Manhattan. Noisy and nuts.

Even now, as the coffee and gin warmed the coldness of my brain and muscles, motorcycle and car engine thunder filled the night. Civilisation on wheels will ruin the world yet. Give it time.

The gin hit me faster than I ever thought it could.

It couldn't have been the coffee. Not hardly.

Suddenly, the leather attaché case before me seemed to *move* a little. Then *stop*. Then *move* again. I shook my head, batting my eyes. There was a curious, slow-motion quality to both those movements. I stared down at the Martini. I had barely reached the bottom of the drink. The coffee I hadn't touched at all. And now a thinly humming and droning sound was filling my ears. The voices all around me, the accents, the low murmur from the romantic kid trying to make the nymphet model, sounded ridiculously loud. Amplified, the way you hike the volume on a hi-fi set. The flesh of my face had become oddly warmer, too. The fingers I stretched out to pick up the glass of gin were so very suddenly clumsy and disorganised that a thrill of alarm shot all through me like a bolt of lightning. An electric shock. I started to get up, to push back from the table. I tried to look around me, to see what had happened. What might be happening. It was like old times, all right, but each time is still a slam into the solar plexus. An abrupt jolt to the mind. An explosion of all logic and nerve-ends. The manhunt and the chase has its price. The Mickey Finn is one of them. Poison is, too. And that's the one thought that paralyses the reflexes, all the motor muscles, as you try to pull yourself back from the rim of the opened grave. The pounding in my ears was now the rushing, roaring, fiercely blasting sound of an express train thundering into a station platform deep below the sidewalks and streets of a city.

The Via Veneto swirled and danced all around me. Frightened, enlarged faces, magnified expressions, bobbed and jumped eerily. The sleek brunette reading *Paris Match* had dropped the magazine, hands flying to her breasts, her eyes round, incredulous pools of surprise and fear. The hot kids alongside me had shouted something, the ample nymphet was gaping at me, mouth popped open, showing she still had some baby teeth. Her swoon-bait boyfriend was on his feet, reaching for me, brown and strong-looking hands clawing out as if he thought I was going to fall. I pushed out at him, too, feeling like a bag of broken glass about to scatter all over the sidewalk in front of the Cafe de Paris.

I did.

But I never saw myself go down.

All at once, like a light switch being thrown, I didn't see or hear another single thing. The world had turned itself off.

I didn't even hear the sleek brunette or the nymphet model scream in chorus. Or the whole sidewalk go up in thunder. And din.

Roma, the Via Veneto and the night, all snuffed out like a cheap candle. A Roman candle, sky-rocketing all the way. And exploding.

The black leather attaché case had stopped moving, too.

That's the rest of the price you have to pay for undercover work. Your eyes play tricks on you.

I'd been had by experts.

★ ★ ★

' . . . patients receiving Valium should be cautioned against engaging in hazardous occupations requiring complete mental alertness such as operating machinery or driving a motor vehicle. That is on the brochure that comes with Valium, Mr. Noon. Therefore I would suggest having someone drive you and take you home when you come for your appointment. If you have any questions, please call . . . '

There was a man in the nightmare. A bland-faced man in a white coat who said he was a doctor. I didn't know any doctors but I did tell him I'd never taken a tranquilliser in my life. Much less Valium which I wouldn't know from Bayer Aspirin. Or a jujube.

Then the man disappeared and another man took his place. A bold-eyed, uniformed, tanned man with bandit moustaches, sitting behind a tiny desk in an office somewhere high above the street.

' . . . she was found before dawn in the very waters of the Fontana di Trevi by the maintenance people who clean the place after the coarse tourists have departed . . . she was drowned . . . very violently. Very brutally. And there are evidences of a sexual assault. Must I say more?'

Captain Michele Santini had come back to haunt me. Accent and all. I told him I didn't kill Joy Deveau. I wouldn't kill any sharp girl, with quiet, good looks. Santini kept shaking his head sadly, his enormous moustaches bristling.

Three shadows loomed behind him and the desk. Hugo, Alfredo and Gino, armed with foot-long clubs.

I groaned and they all vanished in a swirl of dreamer's fog.

I saw Joy Deveau. Exactly the way she had looked that dark night with the mammoth Pantheon rising behind her slender silhouette like some fantasy out of the past. Joy had really enjoyed the cokes I'd bought her, downing them like they might have been champagne. I saw her jeans, green jersey, love beads and long unkempt blonde hair and the rimless glasses perched on her retroussé nose. A little Gloria Steinem roaming all over Europa on her own. But with infinitely more courage and common sense. She knew an awful lot about the Pantheon, too. Not the sort of thing you find only in guide books.

'. . . it's easily the most perfect of all classical monuments in Rome, Ed. Agrippa, if she was anything, was a great lover of beauty in architecture. Think of it. Whole centuries before Women's Lib . . .'

Why would anyone want to rape and kill such a girl?

I tried to see the faces of the two other women who had been found drowned and violated in the fountains of Rome.

I couldn't. Corpses in the water are glazed over. Bloated.

I'd never met them, either.

I'd never even seen their pictures in the papers.

Another groan and another parting of the mists and vapours. Joy Deveau faded back into the dark beyond of yesterday. And memory.

Flood's voice came muffling out of the vast darkness. High and angry with me. Almost shaking with rage. ' . . . you're not funny! Really, Mr. Noon. This is a very serious piece of government business all around. If you would only realise . . . '

His voice wound down, like a dying record on a player.

And then I saw him.

Mr. Flood. Of the United States Embassy.

In the nightmare, he was running, of course. Running as he had in real life.

Raglan sleeve, four-button coat flying, attaché case bouncing, bald head shining. I saw the half-lit façade of the Trinitá dei Monti. I saw the ice cream truck, the customers, the big pizza moon, the set-piece of the Spanish Steps atop the Piazza di Spagna. I heard guitar music, too, and the air was filled with the lusty shouts of natives and the sleepy Roma currents of life. And then I saw the girl. The phantom woman with the long dark hair, the tightly-belted floppy trenchcoat. The faceless female. And I also saw the machine gun. In the nightmare, it was a huge Thompson sub-machine gun, but that might not be true, of course. I hadn't seen the gun at all. I'd only heard it. Chattering insanely.

I heard it now, too. Under what was now only a paper pizza.

Stuttering like a typewriter, bursting like depth charges, sounding off like a field gun. Destroying everything in a red ghoulish haze of Death. The seven figures jerked and tumbled, staggered and fell. And the nightmare went around and around and I went with it.

Up, up, up. Until I thought my head would explode.

It didn't. Because it had nowhere else to go.

The nightmare lurched to a full stop. On a dime or a *lira*.

With the same abruptness and lightning-swift speed that it had begun. It was almost like being spanked into birth by that very first doctor in any man's life. Or any woman's.

Someone had slapped me, too.

Hard across the face, using each cheek for a landing pad for two forceful, punishing, open-handed slaps. My head rang like the big gong on the opening credits of Gunga Din.

Reverberations of fear and surprise set up deafening choruses in my head. Rolling around like charging, clanging fire trucks.

'Come on, you bastard,' a harsh, female voice grated close by, literally punching out the nice words. 'Snooze time's over for you, man. Rise and shine now. We're all out of rainchecks. You know what's good for you, you'll quit stalling and open those baby browns, honey. Come on, now! Wake up. Kate Arizona wants to talk to you — '

She was still slapping me when I opened my eyes.

I had to before she knocked my head clean off my shoulders.

She proved to be just the girl that could do it, too.

7

The Field Of Villians

'How can a nation that belches understand a nation that sings — ?'
— Fortunio Bonanova as the Italian general in Five Graves To Cairo.
(1943)

It was dungeon time in Roma, all over again. Noon, A.D.

I've been down the track too many times in the Unconscious League, to be able to re-act any differently. It's always pretty much the same. They knock you out in one place and you wake up in another one. The real wonder of it is that my brains aren't permanently scrambled or my senses thoroughly dis-oriented. There is no fool quite like an old private detective. Concussions or sleeping pills, it doesn't matter. Smart apples should know better.

This time there was a woman called Kate Arizona.

And a dark box-like room with wood and plaster walls looking like two-months old gingerbread. There was a hurricane lamp on the floor in one corner, shooting an amber swathe of illumination. Just enough to see by. What I was seeing wasn't exactly heartwarming.

My head felt like a crowded, cotton-filled hornet's nest but there wasn't any time left to worry about that. The sand was down.

The woman who called herself Kate Arizona looked like she couldn't have cared less. I didn't ask her. I knew she didn't.

Warm breezes filtered in through an oblong aperture behind her somewhere that must have passed for a window. There was no glass, no bars, no anything. Just a solid opening through which some stars and the ample rays of the moon were visible. I didn't know where I was but it certainly wasn't the Via Veneto. This seemed more like country, with some puny prison in the middle of nowhere. Maybe not even Rome.

It took racing seconds to know that my hands were bound behind me and my legs laced at the ankles. In both cases, it seemed like strips of torn sheeting had been used. Not that it mattered too much. They had dumped me unceremoniously on the hard stone floor waiting for me to come to and they had nothing to worry about, really. I say they because the woman sitting before me, literally lording over the scene, had a machine gun idly laid across her lap. And behind her, a blocky figure of a man stood, as if he were waiting in the half-darkness for a signal or a command of some kind from the woman. The man was motionless.

The woman had to be in charge. It stuck out all over her.

Not just because of the machine gun, which I could now see was that familiar, ugly old destroyer, the German Schmeisser, the most used submachine-gun of War Two. It's compact, streamlined, easy to carry and thoroughly murderous. I didn't have to remember Nazi Europe to know that, either. I'd had a perfect demonstration on top of the Spanish Steps. The woman on the chair, a three-legged stool that might have sat before a piano, wasn't wearing a trenchcoat anymore but she had to be the girl in the gloom with the long, dark, flowing hair.

The Schmeisser had a thirty two rounds magazine, when loaded.

Kate Arizona had obviously emptied it in front of the Trinitá dei Monti. But a fresh magazine, long and lethal, shone in the glare of the hurricane lamp. The gunmetal grey was somehow ghastly.

She had stopped slapping me only because I had opened my eyes. She inclined backward on the three-legged stool, surveying me with some grim sort of inner satisfaction. Time enough for anxious moments to do a once-over on her. But once-over would never be enough for the Kate Arizonas of this world. She was as unique as the Sistine Chapel though the analogy is distinctly paradoxical. There was nothing saintly about the woman. Rather, she could have posed for the devilish *bas-reliefs* on the Doorway to Hell. If there is such a door.

Such a masterpiece.

Even sitting down, with the machine-gun cradled across her lap, it was screamingly obvious she was more than six feet tall. The squared width of her shoulders, the enormity of her bustline bursting under the confines of a black, turtle-neck jersey and the jutting prominence of her knees encased in sausage-skin tight matching jeans more than indicated great size. Black, calf-length boots, with fantastically thick heels, were riveted to the dark floor like stanchions. But even if all that weren't enough, the woman's face said it arrogantly, regally and vulgarly. Like a neon sign announcing a new restaurant being opened. *I'm Kate Arizona, fellows. Look at me! Try pushing me around!*

The face staring down at me with pure Woman's Lib hatred for the last of the red-hot male chauvinists, was frightening. Mask-like.

Her triangular face mounted with a bold, hawk nose and full-lipped carmine mouth with cheekbones stolen from a Medici statue and a complexion that shouted of Indian blood of some kind, was a replica of a warpathing Apache at massacre time. I tried to hang onto my nerve. Apart from anything else, the long, dark flowing hair, practically reaching down to her hour-glass arched hips, was the final barbaric, pagan touch that made of her whole façade one staggering female valentine. She was a woman, all right, but more than that, she fully suggested the brutal strength and rock-like bestiality of a savage human being. What had happened on top of the Spanish Steps would be fly-swatting to such a woman. Nothing more, nothing less.

I knew that too as I shifted around on that dark floor, trying to tighten my muscles and gather my loose nerve-strings. The shadowy figure behind Kate Arizona grunted something that sounded like '*Allora*' and Kate Arizona nodded and placed one of her enormous hands on the butt of the Schmeisser. She was staring down at me. Her eyes told me all I might ever want to know. I was no more than another fly to her. And I had a snowball's chance in Hell of not melting into nothing.

Her eyes were violent, stirring. They never seemed to keep still. As if she was always thinking. Was always furious. And unkind.

'Where the hell is it, you sonofabitch?' she suddenly hit me with the question in a voice somewhere between a roar and a rasp. One booted foot kicked me smartly in the right thigh, making a cramp with astonishing speed. Instant charleyhorse. I put my teeth together.

'You ask real nice, lady,' I tried to smile. 'Where is what?'

She looked like she wanted to kick me again but suddenly she smiled. An Ilse Koch-Death's Head smile and nodded again, as if to herself. An incipient laugh rolled around behind the big chest.

'Okay. We'll do it your way. Just once. And then we'll do it my way. I'll give you that much chance to think it over. Now, from the top. You made a deal with Flood. He brought his attaché case and you brought yours. You were going to swap. Okay? You following me? My cue to horn in on the party. But there's a catch. Flood plays games. Or he didn't trust you, either. His attaché case was filled with the wop telephone book. Got that? And yours, you sweetheart, well, you must be saving day-old Dago newspapers. Check? Check. So okay. Flood double-crossed you, I figure. He didn't bring those documents that we're all so fired up about. But maybe he was just playing it safe. Maybe he wanted to be sure of you. See you first before he handed over a key to a locker or something. Maybe directions to where the papers are. Anyhow, brown eyes, I see it that way. And what I see that way, I follow through on. Flood's dead, right? He can't tell me anything. But you — sweetheart. You're here with me. Kate's real sweet on you. But you got to talk. To tell me things. Or old Kate's going to have to start bouncing you off the monuments. You *do* understand me, Mister? Or do you think I'm just a big girl who likes to talk up a good fight?'

The news hit me harder than she knew. I tipped my hat to dead Mr. Flood. He'd had more brains than I thought. But the news left me exactly nowhere. Deep in the soup. And there was no spoon up my sleeve.

'You don't have to convince me,' I said. 'Just tell me why you chopped down those people — maybe you hate people who like ice cream?'

A surprised frown made her cruel eyes jump into another mood. For a moment, she stared down at me as if I was insane. And then she lifted the Schmeisser from her lap as if to demonstrate it for me.

'Damnedest thing, cowboy. Wouldn't have believed it could happen. You know this thing wouldn't shut up? I wanted nobody but Flood and maybe you for extras in case you got too close. But this damn toy got away from me. Ran like a bucking bronco in my hands — '

'It can do that,' I said coldly, 'if you've never handled a machine gun before. So you wasted seven people to get Flood and that attaché case. That's pretty damn lousy if you ask me — '

'Nobody asked you!' she bellowed, eyes jumping again, the Schmeisser suddenly levelling at me with angry speed. 'You just answer my questions. No sermons from you, boy.'

'No sermons,' I agreed. 'But you're barking up the wrong boy. I was just running an errand for my Uncle Sam. I didn't know what Flood was bringing me and that's Gospel. In my kind of work, they never tell errand boys anything. How did you let him gallop ahead of you like that, anyway? You could have caught him long before he got to the church on time. And left that crowd alone.'

Kate Arizona leaned from her chair, letting the Schmeisser dangle alongside one of her incredible hips. She moistened her red mouth and gave me the once-over this time. Her expression was odd.

'He was nuts, that's what. We were waiting for you to come out of the woodwork. We knew he was meeting a contact man. That part was easy. So I handled it myself. But the dumb bastard had no sense. I jumped out of an alley, stuck this in his face and asked him real nice for the bag. So what does the jerk do? Turns and runs like a wild hen. I didn't catch up to him until he hit the lights around that church. No need for all those folks to die. But that dumb Flood had to play hero. What the hell for? A crummy bunch of papers!'

'Sure. A crummy bunch of papers. And here you are and here I am and your boyfriend back there in the shadows is the bashful type but he's here, too.' I shook my head as trapped as I was. 'Where are we anyway? The condemned man has a right to know.'

'The Roman Forum,' Kate Arizona snarled, 'but that doesn't mean I want to hear any speeches from you, Noon. Got that? You just start telling me where those documents are. It's nice and dark and quiet out here and all the tourists are back in their beds in their hotels. And just to let you know how little chance you have of the cavalry coming in the nick of time to save your ass — there's no guards or cops around these ruins, it's darker than a bat's gullet and there's even a nice little pond out there where they used to drown the Vestal Virgins in the good old days. So you don't want to go for a cold, long dip for keeps, you better come up with some good answers for me.'

'*Et tu, Noonus,*' I murmured and she glared down at me.

'You cracking funny, pal?' The Indian-hued face was livid.

'No way. There isn't a laugh left in me. I was just thinking about Caesar, Brutus and all those cats. And me without my toga.'

'You think about something else,' she glowered, moving the Schmeisser up again in her big hands. 'Like those documents.'

'Kate,' I said. 'May I call you Kate? I swear to God I don't know where they are. Maybe if you told me what they were, or what they're supposed to be, I might think of something. My President, he doesn't tell me anything. It's a lousy arrangement, I know, but that's how it is. I'd tell you in a minute if I could — '

'Noon, you're flirting with Death — ' Sheer venom edged her tone.

'I believe you, Kate. Remember, I've seen you in action. You remind me very much of an old mass murderer I used to know — '

She got up from the chair, red lips pursed in a snarl, face worried and drew back her right leg to give me a crushing boot into the face. I twisted my head, trying to scramble over on my side but the blow never came. Suddenly, the shadow in the background had stirred and a very familiar voice filtered almost lazily out of the darkness.

'Prego, signorina. You are wasting your time with him. It is his method of combating his fear. To be smart, to make the jokes. But were you to ask my advice, I would tell you this is all for nothing. Signor Noon is not an imbecile. If he knew, he would tell us, I think. It seems the United States is as guilty as the rest of us. They keep their secrets, too. Even from the very men they assign to the task. Ah, *que cosa significa* — !'

'You shut up,' Kate Arizona barked, revolving on her stool to hurl the challenge at the man behind her. Even as I rotated full-face in the direction of the voice, straining to see the moustached kisser of Captain Michele Santini, a thousand bees were buzzing all around me. 'You're the damn smart one, aren't you? You had him under lock and key trying to break him your way and it didn't work, did it? We had to let him out so he could make the contact with Flood. Well, up yours, you guinea fuzz. I still had to take over but by Christ, I'll handle it from here on in. Don't worry about the cowboy here. He'll open up like a hot virgin when I start using the pliers on his pubic hairs. Just you wait and see. Nobody's ever stood up to that one and neither will this slob. Stand back, Santini, and watch him blab.'

'*Signorina*, no insults please — you go too far — '

The Schmeisser leaped in her hands, cocking with a metallic click of the bolt. Kate Arizona's mighty height and tremendous size would have made John Wayne think twice. Santini who had come forward so that his swarthy Romany face was revealed in the glow of the lamp, recoiled a step but an angry line throbbed at the right corner of his mouth. Kate

Arizona was almost a full head taller. Santini's uniform was gone with the wind, too. He was now dressed in a plain brown suit with foulard tie. He never looked handsomer. Or more Italian. The very slight corporation, visible in Captain's uniform, was hidden in a suit.

Mastroianni incarnate, now.

'Butt out, Santini,' Kate Arizona boomed in a low voice that was about as intimate as a bull fiddle in the middle of a crescendo. 'If you want to live to eat more spaghetti, you'll do it my way.'

'There is no need for name-calling, woman. Nor can I endorse these tactics you so carelessly employ. *Madonna* — to kill so many persons is — barbarous.' Santini was afraid of her but he was holding his ground. Seldom have I admired a man more. Both for his words and his deeds. Kate Arizona threw her head back and laughed, still pointing the Schmeisser at him. 'Are we animals then, *signorina*?'

'Sure we are, you Catholic hypocrite. But you like the money, don't you? Just remember the price and what's in the kitty for all of us when we hand over those documents and maybe you won't worry your fool head about people, huh? Fifty thousand dollars apiece, Santini. And double that — if we get the documents before Saturday. That was the deal. That's still the deal. Now — do you still want to take Noon's word for it? That he doesn't know anything, that's he's an innocent little lamb with no brains at all? Don't make me laugh, Santini!'

Captain Michele Santini did not want to make her laugh.

He wanted fifty thousand dollars.

Double that too, by Saturday. If he and she could work it.

Suddenly, he no longer cared about my well-being. And why should he? It was clearly not the world he had made. Or wanted to make.

'*Allora*,' he muttered, squaring his broad shoulders resignedly. 'We are, as you say, still in this together. Yet, do me the courtesy of refraining from these very biased remarks of yours about my country, my people. I do not like them,

116

Signorina Arizona. They make my blood boil. And it is foolish of you to anger me. So do we understand each other? It may seem a small thing to you — '

'Sure, sure.' Disgustedly, she waved him off and turned back to me. 'Wouldn't want to hurt your feelings for the world, Santini. But get me those pliers from my bag in the corner, will you? Time's wastin' and I'm dying to find out what this big, strong cowboy owns. Looks like a good stud but you never know for sure until you got your two hands on 'em — ' The relish in her voice was unmistakable.

I closed my eyes for a second, trying to think.

Trying not to think.

If I'd had any doubts about her brutality, they had faded fast.

I was caught in the dead centre of a very bad, very unfunny joke, one that could begin, *a funny thing happened to me on the way to the Forum . . . a stone's throw from the Temple of The Vestal Virgins.*

Happened to me with pliers.

'You know, Noon,' Kate Arizona

jeered, chuckling hellishly as Santini made some rustling noises in a far corner of the little room, doing her bidding, 'I've never seen a Mickey Finn work so fast. Wasn't more than a lump I dumped into your first drink when the waiter came by my table. I'd stopped there to catch my breath, too, realising what a gag Flood had slipped over on me. Wasn't any trick at all to tell all those Via Veneto bastards you was my sick boyfriend. I got you out of there in jig time, too. Santini was parked just across the street, waiting for me in his station wagon. Guess things worked out pretty well for me, all around. Getting you makes all the difference there is, cowboy. Otherwise this caper would be a rotten mess.'

'What makes you think it still isn't? I told you. I don't know anything about those documents you want. You're wasting more time.'

I'd never been more earnest in my life but she wasn't listening.

She laughed louder at that, a jarring crash against my eardrums.

'Then we'll sure as hell find out right away, won't we? Maybe just about four plucked hairs from now. Huh? There's a bundle of alfalfa in this for me, kiddo, and you ain't the jasper who's going to keep me from getting my mitts on it. I want out of this goddammed Roma and those papers are my one-way ticket, Noon. You think that over.'

Kate Arizona's wickedly venomous face was a photograph from the Inferno as Captain Michele Santini handed her the pair of pliers. Sadly.

They gleamed cruelly in her strong fingers as she transferred the Schmeisser from her lap to the stone floor. Glinting jagged teeth.

She clicked the jaws together for effect and the message was very clear. The ugly grating, rasping sound was an overture to agony.

A prelude to all the personal hell there can be.

And there was no way out, either.

No way at all.

It was midnight in the Land of Villains.

Where vestal virgins were buried alive

when they broke their vow of chastity. Losing more than just their special privileges.

I wasn't a virgin, certainly. Sometimes, I think I never was one.

But I can scream just as loud as anyone else. Maybe louder.

And die, also.

Just like everybody else.

I can do that bit, too. As we'll have to someday. All of us.

I'd always wanted to pick my own time to do it in, though.

Kate Arizona wasn't going to give me that chance.

She wasn't going to do anything but get some ghoulish kicks with a pair of pliers while she dreamed dreams of fifty thousand dollars dancing around in her mean, unforgettable head.

If I wasn't a grown man, I would have cried.

Out loud.

Nobody would have heard me, though.

Like the lady said, Roma was asleep.

Tourists and all.

And the recent edition of the Games

was about to begin.

Kate Arizona's Games.

The Tournament of the Testicles.

Me against the pliers.

'*Andiamo*,' Santini said in a curiously dead voice, 'do what you will, *Signorina* . . . '

Or, *Let's Go, Kate!*

8

The Colosseum Caper

'Rome wasn't built in a day.'
— legendary.

I had to do something, though. You always have to do something. No matter what. Or else we're all just a bunch of poor jackasses who have absolutely nothing to say about what happens to us. With no control over the cards that fall our way. Kate Arizona had given me five mis-matching pasteboards, no two alike, not even a flush in spades. She held all the aces. The Schmeisser, the situation, Captain Michele Santini and my fair body. I was lying in on a rigged game, with no chance of winning, but there is something in me that never will sit still for Terror and Death.

Or Brutality.

With or without .45 Colt automatic, I'm dangerous.

Always a threat.

I rolled around on the floor, forcing myself half-erect by shinnying up on my haunches, using my lashed arms and legs as levers to accomplish the contortion act. Kate Arizona watched me with cold and curious satisfaction, towering upward so that her dark head almost touched the low ceiling of the room. There was a bated, fixed and ominous set to her hawk face. Her full red lips were closed together in a fierce biting arrangement. The tell-talesigns of sadism or voyeur's pleasure at the wriggling of her victims. Full-length she was a monstrous shadow. Behind her, Santini's solid form was like a Mutt and Jeff contrast. Santini seemed frozen in ice. He was motionless again. An on-looker who might not condone what was supposed to take place but clearly would take no action to stop it. The Schmeisser rested against one of the three legs of Kate Arizona's stool. The pliers dangled with limp reality from the fingers of her powerful right hand. For a long moment, nobody was talking. Everybody was just looking at me, as if wondering what I was going to do next. The night was young, obviously, and Miss Arizona was in no hurry anymore to start counting my short hairs.

A warm wind fanned in through the rectangular window. The hurricane lamp, protected by glass and metal, did not bat an eye. The clustered stars still twinkled but the moonlight had moved a little. Nothing sounded from outside. Nothing at all. Not even a passing jetliner. The Forum probably had never resembled a cemetery more.

Breathing hard, holding my lashed hands as a brake to the floor beneath me, to remain sitting, I stared up at Kate Arizona.

She stared right back at me, enjoying every insane second of the situation. Maybe revelling in the prospect of unclothing a man. Her eyes gave her away even more than the carmine mouth did. She was in full fly, now. Exposed in all her brutal glory. Perversion, as well as greed, ran whatever motors she owned. I kept that in mind as I launched into the last remaining fight left in me.

The gleaming pliers flexed in her hands, suddenly. The metal jaws clicked impatiently as she made snipping motions with it at the empty air between us. As if I hadn't got her message already.

'Kate, listen to me — '

'Scared, huh? Stewing in your own sweat. Well, go on, condemned man. I like to hear 'em squeal before the party starts. More fun that way. Unless, of course, you suddenly decided you know a helluva lot more than you did. That happens sometimes, too. Guy all of a sudden, quick like a rabbit, remembers everything. Including the name of the first dame he ever tattooed way back when. You were saying, Noon?'

The gloating, almost lascivious tone of her words put nails under my steaming skin but I kept my head. Panic would spoil it all. Captain Santini coughed in his patch of darkness, as if he was embarrassed. But still not embarrassed enough to forget about the money.

'About Flood,' I said. 'You chopped him good, all right. Never saw a guy so bullet-riddled. But he did manage to get out a few words before he died. Maybe you saw me reach him. Maybe you didn't — '

She snorted. The sound was a fire-cracker going off in the small room. 'You bastard. I knew you were holding out! I saw nothing after I grabbed that case and beat it. All I wanted to do was get out of there. So Flood talked, huh? Then he *did* tell you something — '

'He did,' I lied, trying for sincerity as if it were the *sine qua non* of survival. I'd gambled that she had to high-tail it in all that shoot-out uproar and she had. Santini was stirring, again. His shadow stiffened, alertly, to catch every lying word. 'He was smart, like you said. Couldn't trust that it would be me showing up. So he dummied up that attaché case. But I didn't know that until you told me. But dying so fast, he took his last chance and told me where the documents were. How I could go about getting them. He just had enough breath left to tell me and then I had all to do to get out of the area myself with all those dead people lying around and the whole damn neighbourhood yelling its head off.'

I took a deep breath and Kate Arizona bent down, thrusting the pliers full into my face. Her mammoth bosom was rising and falling in the black jersey. Mingled disappointment and satisfaction were waging war somewhere inside her. You can't play your bestial games with a man who you want to tell you something you want to hear. Have to know. I was banking on that, too.

'Go on. What's the rest of it?'

'That's it. I know exactly where the papers are. How to get them. But if you touch one part of me with those pliers, you're not going to know. Fact is, you need me walking and healthy to get your hands on them. That's how the *tortoni* crumbles, baby.'

For a long, painful moment, she was mad. Madder than anybody can be without doing something about it. She cursed, balled her free fist threateningly, twirled the pliers, cursed again and then to work it all off, nudged me none too gently with one of her cruel boots.

127

'A bluff,' she snarled. 'How do I know it's not a bluff?'

'You've still got the gun, Kate, and the pliers. I'm still all tied up for delivery. You can't take a chance, can you? Think about the money you want. You and Santini. And Saturday's double bonus. What have you got to lose except a little time? All I can tell you is you work me over with those pliers and you'll have to kill me before I say a word. Only fair to tell you I have a very high pain threshold. On the level. I kid you not. I can take plenty. And I'd force you far enough to kill me first. See what I mean?'

'*Signorina*,' Santini murmured, but cutting in quickly, all the same. 'He speaks good sense. What he says is true. I know his sort of man. He will bear much before talking. Let us deal with him. As he himself says, there is little to lose. Only time.'

'*Bravo*, Santini,' I sighed. 'You'll be a Major yet.'

Kate Arizona snorted again. But she had stopped swearing, at least. Once more, she peered down at me, trying to read my face. Then she straightened and tossed the pliers away. They skittered across the floor, clanging hollowly. Reaching down, she swept up the Schmeisser and aimed it dead centre at my heart. No bore ever looked bigger.

'All right, all right,' she growled sullenly. 'You got your time, cowboy. And you better make it good. There's other things beside pliers for four-flushers. I'll put your balls through a meat slicer if this is a trick. What do we have to do get those papers?'

I kept the triumph out of my face, controlling a surge of relief so warm-blooded and torrenting, it felt like the thunder of bongos in my veins. It was poker, for sure. Bluff like hell with your pair of crummy threes. But it had worked, dammit. Worked like a Swiss clock.

'It's your lucky night, Kate,' I said, 'in spite of your lousy opinion of things. Those documents are so close to us right now, you'll have your hot little hands on them in no time at all.'

'Spell that out,' she commanded warningly. 'And toot sweet. I've had about all the funning around I'll take from you, Noon.'

'Who's funning with you?' I showed her a fool smile to take some of the sarcasm out of the remark. 'All we have to do is walk out of this little nest about a thousand yards down the road and *voila* — those documents you want so very badly. You won't tell me what they are, will you? Why they're worth so much on the open market?'

'No, I won't,' she snarled. 'You tell me just what you mean and stop clowning around. What the hell are you giving me?'

Santini had moved further into the centre of the room so that he was almost directly abreast of her, matching her absorbed stare down into my face. For a second, both their watching faces were a study in the dazzling appeal that money has for certain kinds of people. Certain kinds of murderous bastards. Bastards, incorporated.

'Untie me,' I said. 'Let me get my

arms and legs working again. You can keep me covered all the way. Flood made it all easy for us. Just a coincidence maybe that you should pick this garden spot for your little party for me. But there it is, coincidence or not. What you want is in the Colosseum. Cross my heart and hope to die. But I can't tell you how to find it until I'm in the place myself. Flood's directions were so crazy I wouldn't know how to tell you to look. Know what I mean? But once we're there and I can fix the location — '

I let that hang, shrugging. Counting on her greed and her partner's to take my co-operation for what it was worth. Old Santini snapped at the bait like it was his favourite Italian cheese. A happy smile creased his face and he forgot himself and poked Kate Arizona gleefully in the side. She jerked at the push but caught herself in time and then shook her head, almost wonderingly.

'The Colosseum,' she echoed. 'You gotta be kidding. That rathole's bigger than a Texas ballpark, Noon — '

'All the same. That's where the

documents are. Do we or don't we go look? Thought you were in a big hurry. Saturday — remember?'

'See, *Signorina*?' Santini chortled. 'Did I not tell you the man would see things the way we wish if only we understand him — '

'Shut up,' Kate Arizona muttered ominously, not growling any longer. 'It smells, that's what. That arena will be crawling with tourists. Even this late at night. And it's pretty dark in there, lights or not. I don't buy this — hiding important papers — '

'I have a flash, Signorina Arizona,' Captain Santini declared dismissively. 'And in any case, it is as Signor Noon says. He has co-operated, he has told us what we want to know. Why do we now hesitate? Why do we delay?'

'Your move, Kate,' I said, simply. 'The Captain's put you in check. Personally, I think he makes a lot of sense.'

'All right, all right! Sold, Mr. Noon.'

Suddenly, she had stepped back, swinging up the Schmeisser to low port.

She might have moved off the cover of *The Nazi Playboy*, in her jeans, jersey and hell-bent-for-leather look. Her cruel eyes pinned me with deadly purposefulness. Her stunning appearance was one for all the books. Dirty books, whip cult manuals and hate tomes.

'Santini's going to untie you, cowboy,' she purred in a low, animal voice. 'Then we'll take that walk. You in the front, us right behind you. There's a path out there that will lead us right down to the Arch, out of all this monument crap. We'll leave the station wagon where it is. Parked on the incline above the main drag. You're right. That cheesebox is close enough from here. But just remember this. I'll be right behind you all the way. One funny move, one piece of funning and Mister you ain't ever going to be good for any woman again. Not ever. I'll fill you so full of lead they'll need a derrick to lift you. I'm not going to tell you again, Noon. You're delivering those documents to us or I'm delivering you to the cemetery.'

'You made yourself perfectly clear,' I

said, trying not to shudder. 'Message received.' Mentally, I was gauging my chances.

'Untie him, Santini,' Kate Arizona directed, stepping back more to get a good view of the proceedings. 'And watch him.'

Captain Michele Santini untied me. With loving alacrity.

As if his life depended upon it, as though I were a holy Roman relic, as if I held the key to his personal dreams of happiness and a long life. Or at the very least, twenty years' back pay in the carabinieri. I wondered where Hugo, Alfredo and Gino were. Probably out busting tourists if they weren't part of their superior's individual pursuit of the almighty dollar. It was hard to say.

Roma has a very curious effect on the senses, all right.

Even as the strips of sheeting fell away, restoring some freedom and blood to my cramped muscles, a line from Julius Caesar raced through my mind, coming at me with random but striking aptness.

. . . the evil men do lives on . . . the good is oft interred with their bones . . . or something like that. My Shakespeare is shaky.

I stretched in the heart of the little room, working arms and legs into responding units. Santini and Kate Arizona circled around me wearily, hawks picking on the chicken slated for the kill.

'Start walking,' Kate Arizona barked, hardly above a whisper. 'And just remember this gun in my hands and what happened in front of that church. It runs away on me — right? Kill the lamp, Santini and tag along — I hope you're right about the cowboy. For your sake as well as his. I've had enough of this horsing — '

'I'll try,' I promised, 'to remember.'

'*Si*,' Santini mumbled, clattering toward the lamp in the corner of the room. She'd given him something to chew on too.

And he didn't like the taste of it. Not one bit.

I started walking.

Out toward that shining Roman moonlight.

And God alone knew what else.

There was more out there than can meet any tourist's eye.

Especially private eyes.

9

Quo Vadis, Noonus?

'Would you have me late for the Games?'
Charles Laughton as Nero in
The Sign Of The Cross, (1933)

The Roman Forum was eerie in the warm moonlight. Under a muggy, star-filled sky, with the round pizza moon in full sail, it was like a trip back through Time. Kate Arizona and Captain Michele Santini probably couldn't have cared less as they piloted me through the standing ruins of Ancient Italy. Under our carefully treading feet, the layers of earth and rubble which had carpeted the Forum for more than a thousand years lay quietly and somehow sacred in the darkness. There should have been some sort of manmade illumination and there was. Huge floodlights, strategically placed for the eyes of the world beyond Roma, threw pale amber swathes of exposure but Lady Kate was having none of that. With the Schmeisser pertinently nudging the small of the back, she was steering a course far away from the circles of lighting, threading our little midnight patrol through clumps of foliage and groves of trees.

It was a cemetery atmosphere. A necropolis of silence. A hush.

Still, there was a world to see. And marvel over. Despite the sticky situation, the panorama had its traditional highspots and focal points of interest. Marble columns rose like tall sentinels along the pathway. Scattered slabs of white blocks, more like headstones and tombstones, littered the area with random solemnity. The pale slate-grey arch looming before us seemed like a gateway or an entrance to the hilly expanse leading down toward the Via del Corso, which could rival the Los Angeles Freeway at any high noon of a Roma day. Behind us, the tri-columned monument which marked the Temple of the Vestal Virgins, poked upward like a grim reminder of the facts of Time and Life. Erosion, wear-and-tear — all things will crumble sooner or later. The-bigger-they come-the-harder-they-fall. All over Italy, ancient monuments, pedestals and statues were beginning to topple on their foundations and bases. Nature always wins the pot, inevitably. Yet, moving slowly and cautiously among those Roman remains, there was no escaping the awesome mood and drama that permeated the landscape. This was the Forum. Caesar had walked here, talked here and was slain here. By Cassius and Brutus and the rest of the jealous plotters who had sought to keep Rome free of dictatorship. You can hardly find real estate like that, even in America, except for Ford's Theatre in D.C. where Honest Abe got his. But here, the stakes had been even higher. A man against a country. The country had won. I had the screwy sensation that I ought to be wearing a toga as Kate Arizona's Schmeisser hurried me along the rocky terrain. Santini was bringing up the rear. There were only the three of us and the fiendish, big lady had used one of the small dungeon-like structures lost among the ruins to house me as her prisoner while she asked all her questions.

She must have known the ground like a native. A *paesano*.

Ahead of our small party, the massive, intended formation of the Colosseum, with its chewed-down outline resembling nothing less than a huge, round drum, lay on the horizon, over the massed shadows of the trees. The Arch of Constantine, just to its left, gleamed and shone on the thoroughfare, an eternal beacon in the night. A way-station separating both halves of Rome. The city half and the country half. Far off to the right, the Palantine, one of the seven hills, rose like a forest of deep green, faintly visible in the hazy glow of electric lighting surrounding the vast dimensions of the great old arena. The dark niches and apertures in the rounded shape of the Colosseum, no longer filled with the statues of Gods and Goddesses, as they had been before the Goths came, showed like cavities. Enormous patches of darkness in the biggest cavity the world will ever know. Or see. The Colosseum of Rome. A Bad Tooth.

The shadowy, still-vivid tableau of the Forum receded behind us. A stone, curving pathway, clean and chiseled, beyond the Arch of Titus, was the last lap of the dark safari through the ancient grounds. I could hear Kate Arizona lumbering behind me. Santini was murmuring something under his breath. We hadn't needed his flashlight yet. There was more than enough light to see by. Moonlight and manmade light. The Colosseum was now only a street away. Just across the shadowy boulevard which, in spite of the late hour, was alive with moving cars and vehicles. We could see an ice cream truck parked before the huge amphi-theatre and two Fiat cabs with their lights on, waiting to pick up some late Colosseum tourists. Stars winked down.

'Hold up, Noon,' Kate Arizona breathed in my ear. 'We got to do this right.' I held up because I knew what she meant. Santini did too. We couldn't march toward the Colosseum with me at gunpoint. There are limits to what the tourist traffic will bear. And excuse.

Kate Arizona had attired herself in the flowing trenchcoat with the tightly-belted middle but more than that, she had brought along one square, black, hard-plastic case with handles. In this, she now concealed the Schmeisser, thanks to the collapsible stock which literally halves its length. Santini kept me covered with my own .45 which he seemed to admire. I knew he had a Biretta of his own because it was tucked in the high waistband of his suit trousers. The snappy *borsalino* adorning his skull was roguishly curved in the Barrymore slouch. It made him a mixed metaphor of time and place, somehow. Such a charming fellow had no business with the likes of Kate Arizona. A lady with a Schmeisser, sleeping pills and murder in her black heart.

'Convenient,' I said, indicating the black case and the now boxed machine-gun. 'Must be your working kit. Like the Avon Lady. You always carry your Mickey Finns with you, too? For emergencies?'

She straightened erect, clasping the case close to her side and sneered at me in the half-light. She looked like a witch, now.

'You bet your ass, cowboy. You'd be surprised how many guys I have to shake off that want to get into my pants. Knockout drops can be easier than wrestling with them though I can handle anybody I want to. Besides, they come in handy — like with you, Noon. Beats pulling a gun on you and kidnapping you in front of a crowd of Dagos at that sidewalk cafe, don't it?'

Before Santini could protest, I did it for him. Mockingly.

'Sure, Kate. You know your stuff. But if there were fifty people at the Cafe De Paris, the odds are pretty good that maybe only ten of them were Italian. That's a tourist trap, lady.'

Kate Arizona's sneer matured into another snarl.

'Knock it off,' she rumbled. 'No sermons, remember? Now just concentrate on what I tell you. We're going to cross that street, go into the cheesebox. All nice and cosy. You in front. Me and the Captain right behind you. He's got your smoke-wagon and I'm heeled, too. So you do what you're supposed to do. And no funny business. And cowboy, you'd better get those papers for me. I told you what will happen to you if you don't.'

'You told me,' I admitted. 'So let's go.'

'Listen to her, *Signor*,' Santini said, almost pleadingly. 'It is foolish to play games, now. You have come this far. Do as we wish. I will not let her harm you. I give you my word on that.'

'Sure,' Kate Arizona agreed with surprising quickness. 'Santini called the shot. You play ball with Kate and Kate will treat you like a king. Who knows? I may even take you back to the hotel with me for a few laughs. Know what I mean? You look kinda interesting. In a way.'

'Yeah. I know what you mean,' I said. 'And it chokes me all up.'

But I didn't believe her for a second. She was Hitler and I was Chamberlain as far as I was concerned. And it was Munich and '38 all over again. Who could trust a dame who chopped people down with machine guns? And didn't even give it a second thought. She was pure bitch.

They didn't all come from Buchenwald, either.

We crossed the wide avenue just where it race-tracks around the huge structure with the Arch of Constantine to our right. A spotty stream of fast-moving vehicles made our progress slow and careful. The hill behind us showing the lofty approach to the Forum was devoid of all tourists or innocent strollers. My mind was busy, accepting and rejecting a dozen different ideas about what to do when we got inside the ancient edifice. Kate Arizona was literally at my elbow, urging me along with a thrust of her big hand. The other one was buried in the side fold of her trenchcoat, probably wrapped around a handgun of some kind. Captain Santini was close enough to her for me to get a waft of some manly after-shave lotion or perfume he might be using. There was no way I could run. Open ground yawned around us in all directions. The Via del Corso which led directly back into the heart of Rome was ablaze with light. I would have been cut down before I got ten feet no matter how fast I could run or dodge. Instant Victim. Like suicide.

It was the Colosseum or nothing, for making my play. If any.

As warm as the night was, a fine sheen of fear dew clung to the flesh of my neck where it met the collar of my shirt. Hotly.

Fiats, motorcycles and little assorted foreign cars careened around the bend, in from the Del Corso as we walked the symmetrical white lines which Rome provides for *Pedone*. Or Pedestrians to you.

Up close, only yards away now, the Colosseum climbed like a skyscraper. Huge, towering, enormous. The dome-like niches, only feet apart, were just so many dark doorways leading into a Never-Never Land of the Past. The storied long ago and far away. But it was the Present that counted now. My Present and my Future if I wanted to have one. Documents or no documents. Still, the shadow of the Colosseum filled what was left of that Present. A Colossus.

We gained the cobbled terrain outside the structure. One of the gaping side entrances opened before us, just like Section Thirty Three at the old Polo Grounds. Designed like the perfect baseball park. Kate Arizona was rigid behind me. Hawk-like, watching, sniffing the air suspiciously like a bird dog. Straggling tourists strolled by, lolling, idling, killing their Roma night with a leisurely, lazy visit to the oldest building they might ever know. There was a murmur of comment audible, words filtering indistinguishably, blending with the motley noises of moving vehicles, chattering Italian cab drivers and then the distant drone of a jet thundering in the sky. I had to wonder what kind of an impression the three of us must have made. Myself, Kate Arizona and Captain Michele Santini. Some trio.

A giant of a female in a trenchcoat, with long dark hair and a square, black case. A picture postcard Italian male, dapper and roguish and one square, solid *Americano turista*. Pictures no artist could ever paint, probably except maybe Michel-angelo. In his cups.

'Which way, Noon?' Kate Arizona hissed at my shoulder. 'This is your party, remember.' Something very hard probed into my spine.

'Any entrance will do. This one here. I have to get inside and see the actual arena before I could decipher Flood's instructions. Okay by you, Kate?' I didn't turn around to look at her.

'Come,' Santini said in a low tone. 'I know this place well. We will be inside in a moment. There's a fine view from this point — '

Captain Michele Santini made a classic mistake. One that nobody who is engaged in the business of manhunting should ever make.

He should have known better. Veteran copper that he was.

Perhaps it was just his eagerness or his

excitement or his anxiety to keep Kate Arizona pacified or just possibly it may have been he under-estimated me. Just that once. A man who had pegged me pretty accurately up until that moment. He simply didn't know how desperate I was because he didn't know that I had lied about Flood telling me anything. Flood who couldn't have told anybody anything.

Whatever the true reason, Santini suddenly stepped around Kate Arizona, took too many strides forward and for a fraction of a second, which is long enough in the manhunting trade, had placed his broad, well-built body between myself and the tall, trenchcoated lady who was also guilty of relaxing her own guard for that self-same fraction of a second. One hand still held the square black case, the other was still jammed in one of her pockets, closed around a gun of some kind. Santini had hidden the .45 in his own clothing somewhere. I've never needed more than a break like that. Not ever.

The trick is moving fast enough when the break comes.

Being ready. Primed for action. Quick to capitalise.

I capitalised on it as best I knew how.

There was no time for apologies or second thoughts. Or manners.

I kicked Captain Michele Santini where it had to do the most good. Right in the erogenous zone. It was a mean kick, a terrible blow to deal out but there was nothing to feel sorry about or forgive, in fact. I had to have him out of the way while I dealt with Kate Arizona. I couldn't have risked a right cross to his jaw that might not have put him out of the picture. Now, he wasn't a consideration, anymore. When a man is kicked where I kicked him, all that man is interested in is sitting down and holding himself together because it hurts so damn bad and he thinks he's coming apart. Any man born of woman.

Kate Arizona had had the gun on me. She was the important one.

As Santini howled in agony, splitting

150

the night with an explosive Roman oath unintelligibly strangled with hurt, Kate Arizona fell back, her right hand flying up from that trenchcoat pocket. A long-nosed, old-fashioned frontier model six-shooter sprang into view. Her hawkish face with its deep-hued Indian colouring went deathly taut. I saw that, too. Faster than the expression reached her eyes.

Cornball though it be —

Death was written in each of her blazing eyes. My Death. Twice over. And dreams of documents and green folding money didn't mean a thing anymore. I'd double-crossed her, I'd been *funning* and that was it, Buster. I was a dead man. The hawk face was a mask of fury.

The gun jumped upward, the trigger depressed and thunder and lightning rocketed around the narrow confines of that side entrance to the Colosseum. The old shooting iron blasting at such close range made a shambles of the sound effects in the ancient amphitheatre. The din might have been a thousand oil drums dropping down a flight of stone steps. All the way down to the bottom. The

Colosseum boomed.

The awesome sound reached me, filling my ears with clanging violence, but the slugs didn't.

I'd turned and dived headlong, away from the outdoor glow of street lamps, back pedalling like a cornered rat through that side entranceway, hopping madly in a low crouch along the circular ramp of a passageway until I lost myself in the shadowed recesses of the structure. Santini was still bawling in pain, bleating like a sheep and the frontier model six-shooter had shut down. All at once. Kate Arizona had fired at least two shots but I couldn't say how many more. Everything was a blur of heart-thudding, noisy, dizzying fear. And the night air was now filling with that different type of sound but still the old familiar one of surprise, terror and confusion.

The same *Kleine nachtmusic* which had gone up when Kate Arizona had mowed down seven human beings. All in an unpretty row.

'*Que fai — !*'

'*Mama mia — *'

'Hey — that's a gun — somebody's shooting — '

'Nah. Just fireworks. These guineas light them up all the time I tell you — '

'MARIO! AVANTI! SHE HAS A GUN IN HER HAND — !'

All that and more. The atmosphere rung with the mad medley of all kinds of voices, all kinds of accents. A symphony of horror.

And then came a more terrible noise. A closer one. Nearby.

The unmistakable clump and click of thick, high-heeled boots rushing down the high-ceilinged little passageway, toward me. Even above Captain Santini's moans of agony, I knew Kate Arizona was coming for me. Coming with all the venom in her big, bruising body.

I raced out from the darkened bowels of the ancient pile of decaying, towering rock and stone into the full circle of the arena. Toward the pale moonlight washing down over the multi-tiered, eroded banks of stone levels encircling the gutted out-bottom of the immense amphitheatre where *thumbs down* had

153

meant no mercy for fallen gladiators. The sanded floor of the arena had long since disappeared but not even the Twentieth Century could change the aura of survive-or-perish.

Kate Arizona was hunting me down with a six-shooter.

I didn't want to be trapped like a rat in the dark of the underground. I needed room to swing. Light to see by. Operating space.

If I was ever going to get out of Roma alive.

To eat spaghetti again. Like Captain Michele Santini.

Or do all the things I like to do.

The Colosseum, which had been Death In The Afternoon, was now the setting for another type of entertainment. A night game for Nero.

Shoot The Running Private Eye.

Watch The Tall Woman in the Flowing Trenchcoat.

The odds were terrible.

Even as I rocketed toward the massive basin of the mighty old death trap, ten million ghostly, toga-clad phantoms rose up from their stone stadium seats, their sweaty, excited faces all aglow, their right arms extended, with every thumb down, rendering that ever-popular verdict: *Kill the bastard!*

It was a full house, too. From the bleachers to the box seats. The natives wanted blood. My blood. Anybody's blood.

So did Kate Arizona.

Ave Caesar! Morituri te salutamas.

Hail, Caesar! We who are about to die salute you.

10

Arrivederci, Sweetheart

*'You shall only be remembered by
the fact that you broke my nose.'*
Michelangelo to Torregiano.

She came charging out of the entranceway. Tall, violent, enraged. Her form
seemed gigantic with the backdrop of
elliptical-shaped stadium. The long-nosed
frontier model jutting from her hand still
looked like it was smoking. But that
might have been only an optical illusion.
She was looking for me, the hawk face
jerking almost comically to the left and
right. And she had the whole damn place
to herself. Whatever tourists and guides
there had been must have vamoosed
like prudes at a Love-In. There were
only small packs of the Colosseum
cats, the mangiest, unhealthiest-looking
strays ever visited upon a public place.

The ancient playground and its environs were literally over-run with the miserable Toms and Tabbies. Great spot-lights, advantageously placed around the curving innards of the arena, flooded the field with illumination. In the whitish glare, the hordes of emaciated animals, frightened by the gunfire, had scattered, too. Running, loping, scrambling for the safety of darkened mounds of crumbling rock. Mewing, howling and spitting all the way.

Kate Arizona still held on to the square, black bag which housed the Schmeisser. But it didn't encumber her at all. It might have been a box of feathers in her huge paw. Nor did she seem in the least bothered by the vocal uproar going up behind her. That awful concert of shouting and yelling. Of people crying out and demanding to know what was going on. She wanted me, that's all. And she was going to kill me if it was her last act on earth. I saw that as perfectly as if I were her own brain. Nothing was going to keep her from doing just that. She came clattering down the stone perimeter, peering quickly and growlingly into each shadowy niche as she passed, poking the six-shooter like a divining rod into every recess. A probe.

I kept ahead of her, dodging and scooting, working warily in the darkness where the floodlights did not touch. But I couldn't keep that up forever, either. It was show-down time. Me and her. So I selected the best possible hump of structure. A jagged, broken arch of stone design angling out from one of the many entrances and exits and climbed. Up to its eroded, clammy crest, some ten feet above the curving aisle down which she would come. Hiding from her forever was not the answer. A thin, skeletal shadow almost gave me away. One of the scrawny cats had picked the same spot to nest in. With a fierce squawl of terror, the animal bolted from the parapet and disappeared into the upper galleries of the amphitheatre. I held my breath, head pounding, and concentrated on the sound of Kate Arizona's boots thudding my way.

She was no more than a heart-beat off.

The click of her boot leather seemed to thunder in the vaulted depths of my shelter.

Each click brought her closer. Lady Cruel, First Class. On the prowl. Until her tall shadow was directly below me. A Big Six silhouette.

I saw her turn, thrust the six-shooter out like she was jabbing a hole into the newest niche in her travels. The moonlight caught her hawk face, curiously softening it but the fiery gleam of her eyes was the same old Kate Arizona. The Kill-Me-Kate character from somebody's nightmares. Whoever had whelped her must have been an extraordinary couple. Babies like her are just not born any old day of the year. Even as I rose, crouched for the jump that would bring us together again, that fatal memory I own, dizzily and crazily, echoed with the words of Broadway at its best. ' . . . *a pox upon the life that late I led. Kiss me, Kate!' Arrivederci*, Cole Porter.

This Shrew needed all the taming in the world, too.

With blood singing, I launched from

the stone pad. Straight down in a compact, striking ball of bone and muscle. Considering her great height and size, there wasn't as much mustard on the jump as I would have liked but it did have something going for it. Surprise.

And true grit. The kind that will make you try anything when the chips are down. Stone Colosseum chips, at that.

One hundred and eighty five pounds of desperate detective, out of New York, hit the big dame squarely. A tremendous grunt and oath of shock and fright, sent an explosive expulsion of breath out of her. Her big, amply endowed figure went down. With me hanging on, knocking the six-shooter from her right hand. She dropped the square black case on her own hook. And I knew in an instant what was worth knowing. She was ready to mix and tangle and lock horns on even terms. I guess she knew what she could do. I didn't. So all I could do was close over her and follow her down to the hard stone ground. In split-seconds, we were both up again, rebounding erect, facing each other. And the battle was on.

I hadn't even put a dent in her. Only taken away her armour.

The gun was lost on the dark earth. The Colosseum abutments and angles and stone conformations, closed us in on all sides. Out there in the moonlight, the arena, with its exposed underground cubicles and cells and rooms, was where the action should have been. But that sandy floor was gone forever. And now the battleground was a cramped passageway along the carved-out circle of the stadium. And the two gladiators, Seventies-Style, was a man. And a woman. And what a woman. Three of anybody else I had ever met. Hands down.

She never lost a stitch. Or a beat.

Quick on the up-take, rapid on the comeback and never stopping to check the runs in her stockings. If she ever wore any. There wasn't a momment lost in indecision or measuring the opposition. She knew who I was and now she knew *where* I was. She came back at me with a flying leap, all the more remarkable for her great bulk. Six feet plus of shapely muscle, all of it contracted into the rage of the woman fooled. Never mind the woman scorned. There's a difference.

Kate Arizona hit me, claws high, fists doubled.

If I expected anything like a wrestling match, a grappling, heaving, twisting, free-for-all, I was dead wrong. She was a Pier Six brawler from the school that pre-dated her by thirty years. More.

She rocked me with a right and a left in almost unbelievable one-two combination delivery. The only reason my head stayed on my shoulders was because I had it tucked down with the chin close to the chest so that no knockout was possible. But my skull rang all the same. Lights danced and shadows thickened with alarming speed. I could hear her happy laugh of cruel pleasure. There was a great feeling of haze in the atmosphere. Instinctively, and only that, I answered back and the cry of hurt and surprise that blurted from her seemed to mean that one of my punching blows had landed somewhere on her bosom. But that too was meaningless. I charged back at her,

162

getting as close as possible, to limit the force of her own punches and it helped me try a few niceties of my own. The close-in school of fighting is just no place for refinements. A man could get killed being polite. Violence breeds its own necessities and hard and fast rules. The major one of which is: *don't lose no matter what, pal. You too, lady.*

She kicked me, then. She knew the rules too and what I had done to Santini she wanted to do to me. I ducked in time and her leather boot jarred into the high part of one thigh. It gave me a fast chance and I took it. I hooked an arm under the boot and flipped with all I had. It didn't park her on her fanny but she lurched, stumbling backward until a poking formation of stone wall checked her big body. I didn't wait but followed up, swinging roundhouses of lefts and rights. I could feel them sinking in. Thudding into her hawk jaws, telegraphing impact up both elbows but I was a wood-pecker starting in on a Sequoia. She could take the best I had and still come up for air. Panic buzzed warningly somewhere in my brain. Kate Arizona was too much for me. I'd need a Mack truck to stop her. Or a gun.

I had neither.

And she now knew that, too.

A gurgling chuckle, dry and like the cackle of a De Sade ready to squash a consenting adult, spread its hot breath over me. I hung on to her, trying to bring her head around in a hammerlock or a half-Nelson. There was so much of her to grab and hold, it was like dancing with a bear, and that too was not funny. Or heartwarming. I wheeled and twisted, trying to bring her around so that her tall body was turned toward the arena. There was empty space down there, just below the protective low iron railing put up for the safety of visitors to the Colosseum. If I could manage to shove her over that, there was hope yet for changing the odds in my favour. I was over-matched.

Unfortunately, she was way ahead of me.

She got the idea maybe the same time I did. Maybe faster.

I could tell by the way she suddenly

shifted, allowing me to rock her forward, pulling her to the rail. She came far too willingly, and in a moment, the table wasn't only turned, it was uplifted. And the table was me. A two-legged table abruptly presented with far different view of the most famous arena in the world. The sky view.

Kate Arizona, powerfully, perfectly, with barely a change in fighting tempo, had lowered her long arms, wrapped them about my middle and rapidly heaved. And up I went, flying toward the sky but just as quickly, she moved her arms and locked them about my shoulder and hip and I was frozen in still life. Abruptly held fast and powerless, my desperately clawing hands useless, as she held me far above her head in the classic conqueror-and-victim posture. For that long and terrifying moment, she savoured the triumph. Almost crooningly.

'*Noon* . . . ' The pant of my name was rich with the taste of sweet vengeance. '*I'm gonna smash you like a bug . . . down there . . . on those rocks and . . . arriverdeci, cowboy . . . '*

'Kate — don't — you'll never get the papers this way — '

She didn't answer me.

She no longer cared.

And she no longer believed anything I might tell her.

The stadium tilted on me as she strained for that last forceful heave that would fling me down into the ancient arena. Which no longer had a true bottom. Only jutting, craggy, bone-breaking, flesh-tearing piles of rock, columns of jagged, eroded marble. The star-studded dark sky, the stone circles and tiers, the multi-niched and recessed old cheesebox of a monument to The Games, whirled and kaleidoscoped in a dazzling succession of shifting, moving stopfreeze views. Balmy breezes washed over me, seeming to pull at my clothes, my deadened muscles.

I was no more than a weathervane in her mighty hands.

The Roma night had become one to remember. To never forget.

I couldn't get a hand free to claw and tear at her, to keep her from flinging me.

She was handling me as easily as she might a child. A weight-lifter couldn't have done better. No way.

And then the world exploded. Careened and disintegrated. Blurred.

Sirens filled the Colosseum. Screeching, wailing, bansheeing, with that frightening meaningfulness that made so many thousands of Jewish hideouts settings for instant Terror in occupied Europe.

Hoarse cries sounded. Whistles shrilled. Cater-wauling. Dinning.

Running, pounding footsteps made thunder of their own. Sounding like a multitude. And then the capper. The big capper. In caps.

The noise to confound Solomon. And confuse God. And mock Mankind.

The Colosseum seemed to explode. To rock with an earthquake. Violent, heart-stabbing detonations went off all over the banked and tiered interior of the vast amphitheatre. Even as powdery bursts of flying stone and rubble and great fiery, smoking flashes of destruction rekindled the dark night, Kate Arizona made her final move. With the stone world all around us beginning to resemble the last days of Pompeii, she gathered up all her strength and sent me soaring out into that chaotic, erupting, upheaval of insanity which the Colosseum had become in fleeting, horrible seconds. The earth was moving, too.

She flung me.

Outward and down. Toward the cruel rocks below.

I sailed into space, heart bursting, brain roaring, senses colliding. The terror of the moment was all mine, now. It belonged to me and nobody else. I had earned it. By bucking Kate Arizona.

Timed with my free fall, came the sound of two other things happening. Things I had no time to consider or think about.

Or translate into English.

A shot rang out.

A single, hammering high-pitched shot. Like a call to arms.

In the midst of all the tumult and the destruction, the shot found a quiet interval of its own and made itself heard. Piercingly.

That and something else. A big something else. The biggest.

Someone shouted. A raucous, amazed Italian blurt of horror.

' . . . *Arcangeli! The Arcangeli*!!!!!!'

There was no more time for anything else. For me.

No more time for sights, impressions, thoughts. Plans.

There was only time for falling.

The worst things in Life are free, too.

Like Noon-On-The-Rocks.

Somebody screamed as I fell.

After that, there was nothing else to hear.

11

Murder la Bella Ragazza

'It's an old Borgia custom.'
John Garfield in
The Fallen Sparrow, (1943)

'The *signorina* is dead, Signor Noon,' Captain Michele Santini announced in his best three o'clock in the morning voice, 'and you are alive. We must begin the discussion we are about to have from that starting point. I trust we will understand one another and behave sensibly. Before we make matters worse than they are, eh? There is much that we can salvage from this affair.'

'It's your story, Captain,' I agreed, 'and I'm in your hands. Seeing as how I'm not going to be able to navigate for a day or two, at least. I would appreciate some facts. I need them before I can do anything about those documents.

Wherever they are.'

I was in a hospital, where I belonged certainly, thanks to three cracked ribs, a badly-bruised femur bone and one awesome lump of hemorrhaged muscle above my right kneecap. When I'd finally come to, there was no Colosseum, no earthquake or exploding stadium, no Kate Arizona and very little memory, either. There was only a small cot in a yellow-walled room with a white metal table at bedside, a little window opening on a patch of darkness, a porcelain pitcher of drinking water and all the aches and pains a man could own without actually breaking anything solid. I only knew what time it was because of an old-style Roman clock on the wall that said three o'clock with its dark hands. And then there was Captain Santini. Still in his sharp brown suit and elegant manner which he wore as well as his official officer uniform. Santini did not have a gun on me, in fact he never looked more hospitable, and the *borsalino* with the Barrymore slouch to its brim, was twirling rhythmically in his tanned hands. Some doctor must have pumped me full of a pain-killer. I was feeling no pain. Just a dim, hazy, flickering recall of sirens screaming, fire and smoke billowing and all that white, crumbling stone at the Colosseum just as Kate Arizona had thrown me away. Down among the ruins.

I couldn't remember the fall at all.

It was as if there was a wall of black between my mind and the fact itself. There were no details. Not any. Temporary shock, maybe.

All I did know, thanks to Santini's fast report on my condition before he talked to me about what had happened, was that I was in the Hospitale Maggiori, somewhere in Rome, not too far from the Colosseum. And the entire situation, the complete set-up, had changed drastically. I was alive, Kate Arizona was dead and Santini was suddenly a good guy again. A miracle of sorts in a city famed for miracles. *La bella Roma.*

There was a lot to think about. And talk about. *Fa subito!*

Captain Michele Santini seemed to be the first to admit that.

'You killed Kate,' I said as if it was nothing more than a weather forecast. 'Is that it, Santini?'

But the question hung like a noose in the close quarters.

The Captain stopped fiddling with the *borsalino* and placed it on the cane chair by the door of the room. Turning, he regarded me very closely, as if trying to read my mind. His midnight black eyes were intent. Then, he sighed wearily. Grandiosely.

'Understand me, *Signor*. So that you do not feel the need to call for help. Or resist what I tell you. A few hours ago I was but a corrupt official fully prepared to do an unlawful thing to earn a good deal of money. But — the *buono Dio* does move in mysterious ways his wonders to perform. Yes, I was that woman's ally, her co-conspirator, if you will, but you yourself saw with what horror I regarded the slaughter at the Trinitá dei Monti.' His theatrical shudder was no less honest for that. 'Truly, a *putana* that Signorina Arizona! But who am I to call her names? Santini — who

173

forgot himself — in his hour of greed. Were it not for the hand of God, *Signor*, all would be very different as of this very moment! It is uncanny — '

'Santini,' I begged. '*Prego*, will you? Forget the roses and string music. What the hell happened?'

'Pardon me.' His smile was noble. His eyes glowed with a sparkle of affection. 'My dear friend — *amico mio* — the *Arcangeli* chose that moment to appear on the scene. There you were — making a struggle of it with the woman because we had pushed you too far — and there was I, a whimpering, foolish official, squeezing his private parts where you kicked in your own desperation — I forgive you for that, too, though it still pains like the very Devil — and then the police were arriving. The sirens, the *automobiles*, the investigators. In a flash, I saw it all. I would be ruined! I — Santini — involved with that woman and yourself in an escapade for money over some valuable papers — ' He rolled his eyes ceilingward. 'I saw my chance then to re-coup. To make it all turn to my own advantage. It was then that I shot the *Signorina*. Exactly at the moments the bombs exploded and the Vatican City squad came pouring into the Colosseum! It was a master stroke. How else was I to justify my being there with the lady and you? Out of uniform? If I could not say I was working on a police problem? One which will not concern the Vatican too much — they do not deal in espionage — '

'Santini,' I said his name as quietly as I could without yelling. 'You're trying to tell me in your flamboyant Italian way — '

'I am telling you, *Signor*, that the *Arcangeli* are no myth! I was not spinning yarns yesterday when I detained you under that ruse about your diary. Those devils are blowing up Roma, as if the pollution, the traffic and the lack of maintenance were not enough. They planted devices all over the amphitheatre tonight. The very night you chose to lead us on a wild goose chase. You were lying, weren't you, *Signor*? Flood could have told you nothing. I went to see his corpse at the morgue while you were unconscious. *Mama mia* — I have never seen a body so riddled. Like a sieve. So — ' The Captain's shrug was a poem of grace and tradition. 'I had no qualms about shooting the lady with my little Biretta. A woman who massacres people so unfeelingly is not the sort of woman for me. So you see — with one turn of the wheel — I restore myself to the side of the angels. I help you, I am considered a smart policeman who apprehends murderers and my conscience is clear. I only wish I could have stopped her before she threw you down. It is a marvel you are not dead but my bullet must have checked her somewhat. You did not fall the full distance into the arena. You merely struck a wall of the closest underground cell and bounced about a bit — '

I could only stare at him. He was the marvel. A wonder of the world where people can deceive themselves over and over again, in the name of some private, personal God. Or conviction. Or principle. But he was a good guy for the time being, at least. I had to settle for that. There was no choice. No reason not to. I was *hors de*, anyhow.

'How bad was the damage at the Colosseum?'

'Two or three tiers of the upper levels. And one wall was collapsed. You should have seen it, *Signor*. Unhappily, the black-hearted *Arcangeli* had placed their devil's bombs and did not linger to see the results. No arrests were made. They must be caught before all Roma falls! What can they hope to accomplish by destroying all our priceless relics and antiques? Truly, it is barbarous.'

'I wish you luck. Maybe they're trying to tell you people something. *When the Colosseum falls, so falls the world —* ' I let up on the quote and changed the subject. 'The woman. Tell me about her. How did you ever get tied up with a she-wolf, anyway? And more specifically, just who was she?'

Santini extracted a hammered silver cigarette case from his inside jacket pocket. Extending a hand, clicking the lid open, his sad smile was attractive and suddenly of a far different stamp. I let him light a butt for me. He was way ahead of everybody. The brand was American and not one of the usual European rope stuff.

'*Signor,* she came to me one day last week. To my own office. And made her proposition. It seemed she knew of yourself and your mission in Rome. She explained to me how I must detain you with a false arrest. She seemed to also know that you were keeping a day-book. She was much interested in the contents of that, also.' The Captain chuckled grimly. 'The gall of the woman! She was so certain I would not arrest her for attempting to bribe me. That I would go the way of all corrupt officials. *Veramente* — she was correct! What she offered — fifty thousand American dollars, you see — made my poor head swim. In all my career, I could never make as much *lire.* Still, it was nothing more than to detain you, examine your luggage, and the diary and then contact her. It was she, you see, who also asked me to release you when I did.

She must have attempted to fool Signor Flood and failing that, realised she must allow you to contact him and then try to intercept the papers — these mysterious documents of which I swear to you I know nothing. *Niente!*' His chuckle changed to bitter sighs. 'Had I but known she would stop at nothing — well, the Trinitá dei Monti was a carnage. And after that, I was deeply involved. Yet it all seems to have come to the proper end.'

'Don't hold out on me, Captain,' I said. 'You're not that stupid. You wouldn't let a strange woman walk into your office, say Yes and let it go at that. Not you. You're too much the fox for that Simple Simon routine. Tell me true, Santini.'

His eyebrows shot up and the magnetic black eyes assumed an air of hurt. Then the expression vanished and he shrugged, conceding the point with genuine modesty. His own brand of coyness.

'You are too wise for me, *caro mio*. It was as you say. I had the lady investigated. Through our Interpol here in Roma. And several other agencies it is not necessary for you to know of. *Si,* I learned much about Signorina Caterina Arizona. Enough to make the blood go cold. She was *una donna diavola*! Never have I seen such a dossiér.'

'For instance?'

He held up his right hand, his own cigarette tucked in one corner of his mouth, his eyes lidded against the rising blue smoke. He began to tick off all the virtues of Kate Arizona by using his left hand to close around each of the fingers of the right one.

It was a report card from Hell. Demerits all down the line.

'*Uno* — she was an assassin for hire. Believed to be the murderer of three officials in South America. Unfortunately, it was not proven. *Due* — she was employed by the Soviet in regard to acquiring some other very important documents relating to the Space Programme of Great Britain. *Tre* — the French government was certain she was the lady who accomplished the ruin and disgrace of one of their highest officials in De

Gaulle's regime through the humiliating process of revealing sexual perversions of the official. There were films and tape recordings of the — ah — acts — turned over to the opposing political party. The official committed suicide. La signorina Arizona was prominently seen in the films and heard on the tapes. *Quatro* — there is a royal family in the Balkans that can no longer hold their pride or their position because each and every member of the *menagetutta famiglia* — have been exposed as users of drugs. Again, the feeling is that the woman Arizona is responsible. Again, nothing proven. But — ' Santini expelled a deep and noisy breath. '*Cinque* — all of this is rather ancient history, *Signor*, dating back a few years but most recently, your own Federal Bureau of Investigation has placed her on their Open File. Which means — should you not be too familiar with your own country's tactics — the lady was to be watched, kept under surveillance — should she ever return to the United States. The charge is relative to the Sedition Act. So you see, Signor

Noon, Signorina Arizona was no lady at all. Rather, she was a most treacherous human being. One whose cruelties only came home to me in front of the Trinitá dei Monti. But now — I am the big hero. I have stopped her. Ended her criminal career. I have let it be known that she was involved with the operations of the *Arcangeli*! Who will think otherwise?'

Again, I had to marvel at his *chutzpah*, his genius for improvisational reversal of fortune. At being able to write me off, too.

'Nobody, probably,' I admitted. 'But what about Flood's murder? And the Embassy. Aren't they up in arms about a dead member of the club? How do you get around that?'

'It is curious,' Santini said, shaking his head. 'They were very much upset, as one might expect. To have a man murdered on the city streets. What is not expected, is that they would be so dismissive about the matter. They seem to be satisfied that the lady murdered Signor Flood and no political inference is being made. At least, in so far as I can make out. Your Embassy has been most sympathetic, from what I have learned through my office, and is not shouting at the Italian government for gross negligence. It *is* all very strange.'

'Strange?' I echoed. 'It's unheard of. There must be more to it than we both know. Especially since I was sent here to get some very important documents. Which everybody is now clammed up about. I don't like it, Santini. It smellls lousy. *Molto stinko.*'

'*Come?*' His eyebrows rose again. He didn't understand me.

'Forget it. My problem. Not yours. Now that you've given up your dreams of getting-rich-quick. Rest on your laurels, Captain. I won't give away our little secret. My lips are sealed. No one will ever know how the great Santini nearly stepped over the line. I didn't thank you for dropping Arizona for me. *Grazia. Tante grazie.*'

A beam lit up his whole face. As if he were seeing the True Cross.

'*Prego.* A pleasure, Signor Noon. But the documents? What do you think of them now, eh? Will you still pursue the matter?'

'I have to. It's my job. But you forget about them, okay? Now, it's between me, the Embassy and my Uncle Sam. I'll think of something.'

'I am convinced of that, *Signor*. Never fear. You are a man who is thinking all the time. When others are not thinking.'

'Why, Captain. That's the nicest thing any cop ever said to me. You make me humble. Almost.'

'It is true, all the same. You are of the Renaissance, my friend, no matter where you were born. There is that *simpatico* of yours — the bleeding heart, I think it is called. You have great humanity, Signor Noon. It is no small thing. It never will be.'

The little yellow-walled room was abruptly filled with an embarrassed, uneasy silence. Santini took his cigarette from his mouth, brushed at his bandit moustaches and exhaled a cloud of blue smoke. All at once, I was aware of the stiffness and slow flow of blood throughout my wracked body. The drug might be wearing off a little. I stared up at the ceiling, trying not to think about Kate Arizona or what I was going to have to do about the United States Embassy mess. Flood was dead but the documents were still around. Where? And how could I get my hands on them now if he hadn't confided in anyone else at the Embassy? I couldn't call the Chief. That was a No-No at all times when the special red-white-and-blue phone back at my office wasn't available. I was the secret operator to end all secret operators. Nobody knew I was alive except the Man. One of the prices we had to pay for exclusivity was that he could never bail me out or send me a CARE package. I was on my own.

From here to the graveyard. And back.

Santini must have read my mind a little bit. He wasn't that far off target when he spoke up again. Almost wistfully.

'Forget about the woman, *Signor*. I know how you must feel about all people. Even the bad ones. But she was no one to bother about now. No family — there was no husband or sweetheart in her dossiér. Or any known lover. In all her thirty years, she was of no man. Not that one. Not truly. She was born in your Arizona of Indian parents. The Apaches? Is that how they are called? And when she came of age, she seems to have run away. To all those countries I spoke of. A wanderer, you see. Homeless, rootless, with no loyalty to any country. Least of all, your America. And her cruelties, this streak of barbarism in her nature. You should see the dossiér! Her recorded acts of sadism are very brutal. She was arrested in '67, in Berlin, because she had tied a young college student to a chair in her hotel room and placed lighted matches all over his body — '

'You can skip the rest,' I said. 'I get the picture. A perfect lady for hire for any country who needed a dirty job done.'

'Exactly.' His voice hummed with agreement. 'The exact sort all totalitarians and Fascists and Communists employ to further their plans for world conquest. An evil soul made use of — '

'Santini,' I said. 'What about those three women in the fountains? Joy Deveau

186

and the other two — do you think — or are you trying to tell me in your own oblique way — '

Captain Michele Santini favoured me with an incredulous frown. His eyebrows didn't climb that time, they nose-dived in a fierce *V* of bewilderment. His dark eyes snapped and his moustaches bristled.

'*Signor*, you astound me. But what have we been talking about? Surely, your own native intelligence does not fail you now? *Ah* — I see that it does — there is something in your face that refuses to accept the cold fact staring you in the eye — '

'Santini, for Christ's sakes — ' The room was too warm, now.

'No, *amico mio*. Don't run away from the truth. It will not go away as you would like it to, perhaps. *Si* — Signorina Arizona murdered the three young women. I did not realise as much at the time but it is all too apparent now. She sought to implicate you, since you were in her plans. She was following you all about the city, she knew of your daybook records. At the Pantheon, she saw you with that *povero cieco* — Joy Deveau. Poor child! She saw at once an opportunity to make false charges against you hold up. So she killed. And killed twice more. The sexual assaults in each case simply justify and reinforce the brutal personality and mind of the woman. Her perversions added to her profit motive. You do understand, do you not? Rather like a blood lust — the coroner's examinations do not reveal evidence of rape so much as they show the hand and heart and mind of a depraved person — '

'Great Christ,' I whispered, 'and Mother of God.'

Santini crossed himself, fervently and hurriedly, as if I had blasphemed instead of revealing my back-sliding Catholic origins. A sense of awe filled the room. Raw and terrifying.

Both of us said nothing more. For a long time.

It wasn't necessary. Captain Michele Santini took off on me.

I never did tell Santini to give my regards to Hugo, Alfredo and Gino. That didn't matter, either. Not any more.

He must have left sometime after I had fallen asleep. The cracked ribs, the bruised femur and the egg-sized lump on my knee, all combined to put me under. I never saw Santini leave the little room. The pain-killing drug worked its points, too.

It must have knocked me out.

Dope will do that.

Dope as well as fatigue and all those other things.

As well as all the brutality there is in the world.

As well as the cruelty.

And the sickness.

And the meaningless insanity.

Of people.

Of governments.

Of documents too important to be sent Air Mail. Or Special Delivery on microfilm. Of the whole dirty business of Espionage and double-dealing.

I slept. The sleep of the troubled, the guilty and the uneasy.

Somewhere deep in that terrible mind of mine was the vague and unshakeable feeling that I had just lived through a scene with the Claude Rains of *Casablanca* and Bogart.

The 'poor corrupt official.'

Be still my brain.

Remembering old movies wasn't going to get me out of Roma with those all-important documents that the President wanted so badly.

Bad.

Maybe, nothing would.

Que sera, sera.

Sing it, Doris baby.

12

The Stone Pizza

*' . . . ah, the cunning! The sorcery of
that fine Italian hand of his . . . '*
in praise of Niccolo Macchiavelli.

It was a morgue like any other morgue.
  Being located in Rome, Italy, didn't
change a thing.
  The dead who come under the heading
of official police business are always
handled pretty much the same way.
Another language, a different country,
can never change the eternal, world-wide
universality of a state of rigor mortis.
Death is death.
  Italian, French, German, Russian,
African, what-have-you, Mr. Flood, late
of the United States Embassy, was cold
like everyone else in the morgue. His
Dead-On-Arrival last stop in Captain
Michele Santini's jurisdictional care was

the same old story. Be it Bellevue Hospital, Manhattan, New York or a Roma basement beneath an ancient police station, the face is familiar. The condition is certified. There were the same tiers of air-cooled drawers which keep the cadaver on ice, the impersonal oak-tag identification markers on the big toes of the right feet. Or left. It really doesn't matter.

A morgue is a morgue is a morgue.

I'd seen it all so many times, smelled that peculiar smell-less smell so often, I moved through the whole affair like a sleep-walker. Or a veteran Medical Examiner who can't let his own heart bleed anymore if he wants to keep on working.

I had a rough idea of what I was looking for.

I wasn't that interested in the personal remains of Mr. Flood. What Flood might have been carrying when he died was a statue of a different kind of marble. It had to be. Or else we're all crazy and I don't know my own trade. Maybe I don't.

In line with the new leaf he had turned over, Santini had given me an official pass to review the remains. And the contents of his person when Mr. Flood was delivered to the morgue. It seemed the Embassy would bury him with official pomp and ceremony the next day. Friday. Bad Friday for Flood. Maybe a good Friday for everybody else in Holy Rome. Again, nothing mattered so much anymore except the simple, far-out possibility that there might be some clue in Flood's effects that would lead the way to the documents. Maybe Kate Arizona had called the shot. Maybe Flood had not been sure of me and come to the meeting with an attaché case filled with only the Roma telephone directory but maybe, just maybe, once convinced he was seeing the real Noon, he might have handed over something else. Something that would point to the grand prize.

The documents. The dingus. The gizmo that the President had sent me across an ocean to fetch and carry. Like a mere gopher.

Hospitale Maggiore's doctors had released me about eighteen hours after they admitted me. I wasn't that much in need of one of their valuable cots and there had to be a lot of sicker folks in happy Roma. I didn't argue and returned to the Villa del Parco for the good night's sleep I needed before tackling Santini early on Thursday morning for the permit to inspect Flood. The good Captain, humming an aria from *The Barber Of Seville* was only too glad to comply. It seemed the bombing and shooting mix-up at the Colosseum augured grand things for his coming years with the Carabinieri.

As for the hated *Arcangeli*, there were a few leads that might land all the explosive rascals in the police net, soon. I told Santini I hoped so and tottered out of his small office on the rather fashionable black cane I had bought on the Via del Corso that same morning to help me get around town. I was limping very badly, thanks to the bruised thigh-bone, taped ribs and stiff knee. No thanks.

Like a Richard Wentworth out of *Satan's Death Blast* by Grant Stockbridge when I was a dreamy kid reading pulp mags by the yard.

'*Ciao*, Eduardo,' was Santini's jovial parting shot.

'*Ciao*, Michele,' was all I had left in me. It wasn't Goodbye.

I navigated on the cane down the winding, cork-screw stone steps toward the basement below the street level of the building. To the grey, grim door that said MORGUE in big black letters and under that the typical Roma No-No — *VIETATO*, which was plastered all over the city no matter where you turned. Almost as many times as the symbol *SPQR* and *that* is stamped in marble, on manhole covers and building cornices.

SPQR. Senatus populus que Romanus. The Senate and People of Rome.

VIETATO. Sort of a *Forbidden, Prohibited and Keep Out*.

There was a morgue attendant. Just one. There always is.

A thin, bald, dull-eyed *paisano* with a

semblance of white uniform covering his scarecrow physique, a crooked, withered cheroot clamped between his store-bought teeth and a copy of something called *Il Mondo* dangling from one hand. He took Santini's official pass from me, scanned it unenthusiastically and then walked me back among the tiers of air-cooled drawers, which always resemble so many filing cabinets, stacked like logs. I didn't look for Kate Arizona's private coffin. I didn't even want the look at Flood. I only wanted to see and examine the leftovers of a man's life. The things he had been wearing and carrying when his body became the temporary property of a police department. The sad fate of all DOA's. All over this tired globe.

The attendant halted mid-way down the line, grunted and pulled back a long drawer by its curved handle. About as high as our ribs. He indicated the large, clear, plastic envelope at the very bottom of the tray. There, next to Flood's bared, tagged toes was the sum total of the personal possessions he had brought with him to the Trinitá dei Monti when

Kate Arizona machine-gunned him into eternity.

I was able to show the attendant I wanted to examine the big plastic envelope and he waved me to a nearby white metal table and matching chair which was placed for just such usage in the aisle between the banks of drawers. Nodding at me and closing the door on Mr. Flood once more, he returned to his post at the entrance of the room, to the left of the grim grey doors. The cheroot was a dead cigar.

It didn't take too long to inventory Flood's valuables.

As I emptied the envelope slowly and carefully, part of the story of his life and personality and times emerged as well.

There was an OMEGA wrist watch so new it might have been bought only last week. Like a birthday present or something.

There was a pack of EMBASSY cigarettes, the English brand, and that pointed to a quixotic nature that might think it cute to work in an Embassy building and smoke a weed with the same name.

There was a small ring with six keys clinched to the circle of metal. Keys seeming like the things for a car, doors, cabinets, files and safe deposit boxes. It was hard to tell.

His billfold was a top grain cowhide maroon beauty and it held roughly twenty thousand *lire* which is actually only about forty five bucks, American. The billfold contained nothing else. Only the cash.

Loose *lire*, all in coin, amounted to no more than carfare and cigarette money. About three dollar's worth all told.

There was an Eisenhower 1971 silver dollar which somehow seemed like a good luck piece. Or a souvenir. Not for spending.

A single red admission stub to the Giardino Zoologico, dirty and well-worn from not being thrown away, again showed a rather lonely man who didn't go in much for company. Like girls and things. When a guy like a Flood goes to the Zoo all by his lonesome, what else can you make of it? Of course, it was just *his* ticket and the other person could have kept their own but it's been my experience when you treat somebody to something, you hang onto the stubs. Not the other way around. Either way, it was meaningless. Worthless, really.

I probed through the pile. There wasn't much left.

A black comb in a leather case. The material was frayed a bit.

A signet ring which showed a University of Iowa graduate, Class of '47. And a nail clipper. Meticulous. Fastidious. Kept clean.

And a small, gold-leaf address book containing far too many names and addresses to make anything of, in a conclusive way, unless I went right down the line and took them all by the numbers.

There was one last thing in the plastic envelope.

Somehow, as I picked it up in anxious fingers, I knew I had what I was looking for. The item was so bizarre, so unique, so unlikely, if you operated from the premise: why would a man like Mr. Flood bring it to a secret rendezvous with a man he had never met, with whom he is going to exchange black leather attaché cases? He couldn't have brought it by a mistake. It couldn't be an oversight. It was too large to carry by accident. It was too specific a thing not to be the needle in the haystack. The gimmick.

The final item of Flood's inventory of personal possessions was a book. And maybe the best book there was.

Or more appropriately, a pamphlet.

A brochure.

No more than 5 × 8 in oblong size, as thin as barely sixty pages could make it, with a slick white vellum cover whose front bore a reproduced drawing of an ancient ornamental vase. The picture bore the signature of the artist. A very famous name who was not famous for being an artist in the illustration league. By John Keats, the sketch declared. For all admirers of poetry everywhere.

The brochure was *A Room In Rome*. The vase was the Grecian Urn.

And it was Vera Cacciatore's lovely memoir to one of the greatest poets of them all who had spent the dying months of his life in Roma sometime in the last century. That Keats. The immortal one who was a contemporary of Shelley and Byron and whose last room is the amazing historic one in the old building at the very base of the Spanish Steps in the Piazza di Spagna. Just above Bernini's *Barcaccia*. The Tub.

The Spanish Steps where Flood had arranged his meeting with me.

Before he died.

My hands must have been trembling as I whipped through the pages of Cacciatore's love letter to her favourite poet. The *Hunter* indeed. I could smell the chase, the game — the end of the trail.

I knew I had run the documents to earth. The Big Papers.

I had.

There it was. Bigger than Life and somehow infinitely better.

On page 14 and the breath of relief and joy I exploded made the thin, bald, bored old attendant jump in his chair. He had been dozing off with *Il Mondo* slipping from his gnarled hands.

I controlled myself, winked at the *paisano* and rose from the table, signalling I was through. With the air-cooled drawer, with the plastic envelope. With everything. I didn't even need to take *A Room In Rome* with me out of the building. The Keats-Shelley Association of America, Inc., New York, which had printed Miss Cacciatore's brochure might never know how they had assisted their government in the performance of high-echelon, top secret cold war strategems.

Page 14 said it all.

Showed the way as clearly as if it were X Marking The Spot.

It was exactly that. No more. No less.

Page 14 showed the interior of the Keats-Shelley Room. The heart of the place in photographic detail. A sharp, black-and-white still which took up half the page. You couldn't ask for better focus.

Under the photo was the identifying caption:

3. THE MAIN HALL
Talking of lovely things that conquer death.

Leigh Hunt.

And Flood had scribbled, in a precise, CPA's sort of hand in black ink — *left of archway, third shelf, behind books — good luck, Noon. Give my regards to the Man. C.D.F.* Across the top of the page.

He would have given me the book once he was sure of me.

Clifford Daniel Flood, as the obituary columns listed his full name in the Roman tabloids that week, had done himself proud. And Leigh Hunt's beautiful line on page 14 might have been a fitting eulogy for him. Like a bugle call or a drum roll.

Talking of lovely things that conquer death.

Nice going, Flood.

I walked out of the morgue almost

forgetting that bad limp.

My veins were singing. Laughing out loud.

They always do when one of the club hits a home run.

They always will, too.

There was nothing to talk to Santini about, either.

When pizza is made of stone instead of flour and cheese and oil and tomato sauce, then and only then will the Santinis of this mad old universe know what it means when a man dies for something he believes in. Or at least, tries to believe in.

It's something nothing can ever kill.

Or stop. Or put an end to. Or wipe out forever.

No, not even machine guns.

Not anybody's machine guns.

13

Bad Friday For the Big Stiffs

'ABANDON HOPE, ALL YE WHO ENTER
HERE!'
— *Dante, The Divine Comedy.*

They were throwing up scaffolding all
over the stone sides of the Colosseum
that last weekend in Roma. Never mind
the dirty pool of the *Arcangeli*, the
old Flavian Amphitheatre had been in
bad shape for a long time, now. What
was happening to the city of Rome
was happening all over sunny Italy.
Monuments, statues, historical relics and
remains, which had withstood the test
of Time and Centuries, was finally
succumbing to the collective evils of
polluted air, too many automobiles,
too much vandalism and the general
attitude of *Who-Cares?* shown by most
of the industrial class who had begun

205

life as Italians but were behaving like buck-hungry opportunists who didn't care about twenty years from now. Or ten.

It was a lot like a bad movie in which the old villain is all too identifiable by his fat stomach and greedy smile.

Michelangelo, Bernini, Da Vinci, Ghiberti and that whole crew of masters were crumbling by the day. The Pisa Tower was leaning dangerously, the Dumo at Pompeii was toppling, the paving stones along the Appian Way were disappearing rapidly and every romantic Roman was dying in the hot, muggy, bleaching daylight. Dying of despair, sadness and broken artistic hearts. An agent for the Committee To Save Rome's Treasures, was quoted in the dailies as saying — ' . . . a country with no respect for its past must truly be a country with no future at all.'

The Pope added his powerful voice to the chorus but nobody paid much attention to him, either. It was all Papal Bull.

That final Friday as I packed what little luggage I had before checking out

206

of the Villa del Parco, I wasn't caring very much myself. Flood was still dead, I had the documents and I was going home. Documents which in their five-page, hieroglyphic-mess-of-symbols state were absolutely indecipherable by me. But that was not my job. The President wanted them and the President would get them. Paper clip and all. There was no cover, no sheaf, no binding. Just five white sheets of bond, maybe 6 x 9 in some screwy kind of code. But there was a signature on them. A very famous signature on the last sheet and maybe that was the crux of the whole matter.

I can't reveal the autograph, here.

Top Secrets can't be much topper than that particular name.

But it gave me some indication why the sheets might not have been micro-filmed or photostated. They were originals and perhaps the holograph copy meant everything. To the President.

Either way, the assignment was done.

Lifting the papers from the Keats-Shelley Room was no sweat at all. Miss Vera Cacciatore was on holiday again and a little after the tall, darkly handsome uniformed guide let me in, I browsed around the Main Hall and heisted the sheets from behind the third shelf books, left of the archway, while he was busy accepting admission fees from an awe-struck, long-haired, cute college girl who couldn't get over just where she was standing. And living.

'Keats,' she gasped reverently to her equally long-haired, just-as-blond boyfriend. 'Keats and Shelley. It's just out of sight . . . '

'Ah,' the boyfriend snorted. 'You read Rod McKuen. These cats can't cut it anymore . . . '

I got out of there before they started an argument.

Downstairs, outside in the boiling, muggy sun, I took a last drink from Bernini's Fountain. The Spanish Steps rose in the sunlight, crowded with the flowers, the tourists, the Hippies. Guitar music followed me all the way into the cab I flagged down to get back to the hotel. The American Express Office up the block looked like a pilgrimage of jeans, long hair and Survival Jackets as we drove by.

I didn't look back.

The President's papers were burning holes in my inside coat pocket. The coat that will never be a turncoat. It isn't built for it.

I can't dress any other way.

There was no longer any need to keep a diary, either.

Or worry about there being any back-up agents for Kate Arizona. She had been working alone and I might never know who had sent Big Her after Flood and the documents. Roma had another mystery.

Santini had returned my .45, too.

There was nothing left to do but travel.

All the way home.

Eduardo Mezzagiorno would take his leave of Roma and all things Italian. Both great and small.

It was *buona sera*, Capitano Santini. And *Arcangeli*.

Buona notte, Death. Screw you, Hugo, Alfredo and Gino.

Farewell to *prego, ciao, scusi, una, due, tre, quatro,* the *Fiats,* the *motocicletta,* the statues, the museums, the hot, baking stone and the *lira,* the *aranciata, gelati* and *capuccino.* Goodbye to the monuments, the *Termini,* the soundless water fountains and the ringing *campanile.* So long, friends, Romans, countrymen and an *Andiamo!* to you, too. No more *trattoria* and *ristorante,* either.

The good old U.S. of A. never looked better to me.

The Via Veneto could stay where it was. In a Fellini movie.

Papparazzi, away.

The sooner the better.

Guarda la tutta, guarda la bene — the old Italian proverb goes. *Watch everything, watch it well.*

I had come, I had seen, I had not conquered. Unlike Caesar.

I was going back home to mind my own store.

Nothing else made more sense.

Now.

14

Spqr — and Out

'Arrivederci, Roma . . . '
— as sung by Mario Lanza.

The jetliner rose into the sunlight like a mammoth steel bird, banked slowly toward the West and headed home. Toward the Pacific beyond France's iregular coast. I settled down in my window-and-smoking seat and took out my Camels.

There was a fine hum to the air-pressured cabin. An undue brightness, a sense of well-being, a quiet feeling of peace. The seat next to me was empty. I made myself comfortable and looked out the plexi-glassed whisperjet window. The world gleamed.

Down below, forty five degree angle of ascension and all, Roma lay like a sprawling, scarlet woman ready for her next lover. Or customer. The whore, lush, wanton and tired, by daylight.

St. Peter's marvellous dome shone in the golden rays.

The Tiber crawled, and turned, and twisted like huge snake between the Vatican City and the metropolis of Rome.

That Tiber. Where Caesar and Brutus swam. All the Roman legions.

And then I saw the Colosseum. Shea Stadium-with-holes.

Spread out, a monster cavity. An ellipse of decay. A mockery. The biggest bad tooth of them all. One that might need filling. Or extracting. If that day would ever come. Could ever come.

But what dentist would take the job? What dentist could do the job? I didn't know. I couldn't say.

I closed my eyes and leaned back against my seat.

Addio, Roma!

Goodbye. Maybe, forever.

I had no desire to go back again.

And the Colosseum — it was only a hole, after all.

A hole in the mouth of Mankind. That

spoils Rome's kiss.
I'll tell Sophia myself.
The next time I see her.
If and when.

THE END